Take charge of your life

VEDANTIC PERSPECTIVES ON TRANSACTIONAL ANALYSIS

INDRANIL MITRA

ATLANTIC
PUBLISHERS & DISTRIBUTORS (P) LTD

ATLANTIC
PUBLISHERS & DISTRIBUTORS (P) LTD
7/22, Ansari Road, Darya Ganj, New Delhi
Tel.: +91-11-40775252, 40775213
E-mail: orders@atlanticbooks.com
Web: www.atlanticbooks.com

Published by Atlantic Publishers & Distributors (P) Ltd 2024

Disclaimer

- The author and the publisher have taken every effort to the maximum of their skill, expertise and knowledge to provide correct material in the book. Even then if some mistakes persist in the content of the book, the publisher does not take responsibility for the same. The publisher shall have no liability to any person or entity with respect to any loss or damage caused, or alleged to have been caused directly or indirectly, by the information contained in this book.
- The author has fully tried to follow the copyright law. However, if any work is found to be similar, it is unintentional and the same should not be used as defamatory or to file legal suit against the author.
- If the readers find any mistakes, we shall be grateful to them for pointing out those to us so that these can be corrected in the next edition.
- All disputes are subject to the jurisdiction of Delhi courts only.

Printed & bound in India by Atlantic Print Services

To

My guides and teachers in Vedanta and
Transactional Analysis,
Swami Parthasarathy and Julie Hay,
And my granddaughter Amyra, age 3 years,
With deep respect, eternal gratitude
And love

Acknowledgments

With humility, I pay obeisance to the enlightened sages who composed the *Upanishads* and the *Bhagavad Gita;* the spiritual masters who explained the philosophical system of *Vedanta* and elaborated on them; the great Swami Vivekananda; his beloved Master Ramakrishna Paramhansa; Swami Bhoomananda Tirtha and Swami Parthasarathy, who set my feet upon this path; Yogananda Paramhansa; Swami Prabhupada; Swami Chinmayananda; Swami Rama; and the other sages and spiritual seekers I learned from, either directly or through their lectures, discussions and writings. I gratefully acknowledge the help I received from Professor Julie Hay, who guided me to her invaluable resource of *TA Then and Now;* the TA practitioners and researchers who worked on the spiritual dimensions of TA, too numerous to name but listed in the References Section; the masterful works of Gary Zukav, Dr. Joe Dispenza and Dr. Bruce Lipton, which showed me that *Vedanta* indeed contained the deepest truths that science was inexorably approaching. My grateful thanks to Manisha and Namarita and the team at Atlantic for all their help.

And above all, I gratefully acknowledge the constant support and encouragement I received from my wife Roopali and my daughters Ipsita and Urvashi. I could not have done this without them.

Preface

Dr. Eric Berne laid the foundations of a new social psychology in the period 1950 to 1970 for describing the human personality. He named it Transactional Analysis (TA) as it was based on the analysis of transactions or interactions (verbal as well as nonverbal) between two or more persons. The term "transaction" has a very precise meaning. When I interact with another person, I am investing a certain amount of psychological energy in my words, gestures and body language, and I expect to get something back in return, that is, I expect the other person to put in some amount of psychological energy in responding.

Dr. Berne built an elegant and scientifically constructed theory of personality that was easy to understand and relate to. Unfortunately, he died of a heart attack in 1970, before he could develop his ideas further. It was left to his colleagues and students to carry on the work he started, aided by the powerful institutional mechanisms that he set up, the International Transactional Analysis Association (ITAA) and the Transactional Analysis Journal (TAJ). Since then, many other psychotherapists, researchers and practitioners have added to the body of TA knowledge so that it now comprises a wide-ranging set of theories about the way people think, feel and act, and what their behaviour means in terms of their mental makeup. Specifically, various schools of TA have emerged, and it is generally recognised that it can be applied in areas other than psychotherapy, such as counselling, education and organisational development.

I first learned about TA in the 1980s, as a young HR management trainee in my organisation, where it was taught as a part of our Behavioural Science training module. I was immediately captivated by its elegance and simplicity. I started following developments in TA in earnest, and later, during a stint as a senior faculty member at my company's management institute, devised a workshop covering significant aspects of TA in a simplified form, with a view to build better interpersonal and communication skills among the trainees. Later, in the spirit of Eric Berne's dictum that TA should be intelligible to an eight-year-old child, I have ventured to make it as easily understandable as possible to the interested reader, in my first book *Winning Hearts and Minds: Transactional Analysis Simplified*. The objective was to make this approach a powerful vehicle for self-development and personal growth, which in a way can be considered as its fifth field of application.

However, since TA remains a work in progress, there are still several intriguing questions for further exploration such as: What if anything lies behind the ego states? How exactly does the Adult ego state function? How can we achieve the Integrated or Integrating Adult? What is the exact meaning of autonomy and can we add or amplify its characteristics beyond what was originally envisaged? How do we achieve it; only by becoming script free or is there something more we can do? What is the nature of Physis, which is still only cryptically defined and what is its logical end?

These questions and others have been addressed by various practitioners and researchers, who in their own way have contributed to the growing body of specialised knowledge over the years. There has also been a long-standing interest in the spiritual dimension of TA, different aspects of which have been explored by several therapists and counsellors, who have put forward various theories about it. In fact, in 2019, the *Transactional Analysis Journal* devoted a theme issue to the subject of "*Transactional Analysis and Existential Perspectives: Religion, Faith, Spirituality and Beyond*".

Earlier, in 2001, I had attended a seminar on *Vedanta* conducted by the renowned Swami A. Parthasarathy. *Vedanta* is an Indian philosophical system that is at least three thousand years old (and possibly even older). At the end of the immensely enlightening seminar, he had presented me with a copy of his book, *Vedanta Treatise*. I requested him to autograph it for me, and he wrote on the flyleaf with a flourish: "Indranil, discover thyself!" signed and gave it back to me. It remains one of my most treasured possessions.

After carefully studying the book and reading works of other spiritual masters, I was excited to learn that the worldview of *Vedanta* provides very enlightening viewpoints for addressing the above TA issues, and also points the way for self-development and, eventually, spiritual growth. Not only that, it also enriches and informs the approach, and should be useful to practitioners in all its fields of application. For the reader who does not have any specialised knowledge of either TA or spirituality, the interweaving of the two will serve as a guide for living a better and more meaningful life and for emotional, intellectual and spiritual enrichment.

I may add that I am not the first person to link TA and *Vedanta. Embracing Eternity: A Psychophilosophical Exploration of Death from the Vedantic Frame of Reference (Suriyaprakash and Geetha, TAJ, 2014)* has previously discussed this relationship. However, the authors are more concerned with death and grieving, and generally focus on the Vedantic concepts in relation to helping people overcome loss and the grieving process and the fear of death. In this book, we will be mainly concerned with living a richer and more fulfilling life, and with spiritual growth.

This book is a development of my earlier paper *Transactional Analysis and Spirituality: Insights from Indian Philosophy (Mitra, IJTARP, 2020).*

A caveat: This book presupposes some basic knowledge of TA concepts. However, I will be discussing only those aspects of TA that are relevant to the above questions and not all the theories that comprise this body of knowledge. Thus, rackets, games, transactions, script theory, imagos, etc., are outside the scope of this book. Readers interested in these can refer to my earlier book or any other introductory book on TA.

Similarly, I will be discussing only those aspects of *Vedanta* that are relevant to my objective stated earlier. Indeed, the ocean of *Vedanta* is vast, and in this book I am barely skimming the surface. But I hope to show how a 3,000-year-old philosophy originating in the land of the sages and the saints, India, describes the complete human personality, including and going beyond TA in its scope, and also provides the most illuminating answers to many abstract questions that perplex us, such as those given above and also questions like "What is the meaning of life?"; "How to live well/wisely?"; "How do I reach my full potential?". It also addresses concerns raised by later TA practitioners such as Ecological TA and the ultimate aim of TA being homonomy instead of autonomy. These are marvellously captured in the Vedantic concept of *Rin,* or fivefold debt, which I will discuss in more detail later.

I have included quotations, examples, stories and personal anecdotes in an effort to make the book more engaging, not only because psychology and philosophy are weighty subjects, but because the light of wisdom is still light, no matter which lamp it comes from. In fact, one of the most sacred prayers in our scriptures is *"Tamaso Ma Jyotirgamaya",* which translates as *"Lead me, O Lord, from darkness to light"*. I will be happy if the reader considers my book as part of this endeavour.

I also wanted to convey the message that we should seek wisdom wherever she is to be found and not confine ourselves exclusively to one or two domains of knowledge. As a matter of fact, I do not agree with everything in *Vedanta* either; my intellect rebels against an important theory in it, and I do not take it into account in my work for that reason. However, to find out what it is, the interested reader will have to wait till the Epilogue!

This book, then, is my humble attempt to repay my *Rin* (debt) to the Supreme Principle that finds expression in the universe, the world and in all of us.

Indranil Mitra

January 2024
New Delhi

Contents

1

The Ego States and the Fivefold Sheath

"The unexamined life is not worth living"

—Socrates, c. 4th century BCE

The Ego States

Transactional Analysis (TA), the social psychology whose foundations were laid by Dr. Eric Berne in the period 1950–70 is, in its simplest form, a mechanism that can decode your personality within a given framework on the basis of your behaviour and interactions with others. It now encompasses a wide-ranging set of theories relating to the human psyche. Although originally intended for the use of psychotherapists for treating patients, it is now well recognized that there are four fields of application of TA: psychotherapy, counselling, organisational and educational. Thus, for example, TA is used to treat people with psychological problems manifesting as behavioural issues. It is used to counsel singles and couples with marital or childrearing problems, as an aid to open and honest communication, to build strong interpersonal relationships and to improve productivity in an organisation, and to build a strong psychological foundation in growing children. However, TA can also be used for self-development and personal growth. This is because simplified TA is easily understandable to the interested person who has no previous specialised knowledge of the approach, but it is TA nevertheless, a scientifically and methodically constructed frame of reference capable of easy validation in everyday experience, which gives rise to countless "Aha! So that's why..." moments.

Shrikant was getting fed up with the backbiting in his team. It seemed like many of his subordinates had a pleasant smile on their face and a knife concealed behind their back, ready to stab their colleagues at the first opportunity. The conversation was guarded, giving nothing away, and they were generally reluctant to share information, acting on the premise that knowledge is power. The departments functioned in silos, and coordination meetings were less coordination and more accusation.

One day, he voiced his frustration to two of his trusted colleagues, "I wish things would function more smoothly around here! I've had it with this bickering and finger-pointing. We seem to have major communication issues and a huge trust deficit"!

One of them said reflectively, "Remember we attended a TA 101 course two weeks ago? Well, it's really made a difference in the way we look at things, including ourselves. I have a feeling that this is just what the team needs, in terms of improving communication and building interpersonal skills and trust. You may like to consider signing up the others for it in batches".

TA holds out several exciting promises: that of discarding self-limiting beliefs we may have internalised while growing up, progressively increasing our ability to respond to every situation appropriately, building close relationships based on mutual respect and trust and harnessing our innate psychological energy for its best purpose to realise to the full our potential for excellence.

As previously stated, TA has expanded far beyond what it originally was and now encompasses a whole set of theories about the human condition. Without going into details, it envisages the personality to consist of three parts or ego states:

The **Parent ego state** contains copies of thoughts, feelings and behaviour we have learned from our parents and other significant authority figures while growing up;

The **Adult ego state** is that part of our personality in contact with the here-and-now external reality (that is, the situations in which we find ourselves at given times);

The **Child ego state** consists of thoughts, feelings and behaviour we have internalised when we were children and particularly significant experiences we may have had while growing up.

These have nothing to do with what we commonly mean by "ego" (he's got a big ego) but refer to a consistent pattern of thoughts, feelings and behaviour.

In terms of behaviour, the Parent ego state is further subdivided into the **Structuring Parent**, which lays down rules and sets boundaries, and the **Nurturing Parent,** the caring, comforting and compassionate part. Similarly, the Child ego state is subdivided into the **Adapted Child,** which consists of the way we adapted to the messages received from our parents while growing up (and in some cases, our interpretations of those messages) and the **Free Child,** which represents the essential unfettered part of ourselves. Another part, the Adult ego state in the Child, which is in touch with the external world in which the child finds herself, is sometimes referred to as the Little Professor.

The ego states are not fixed and static in themselves but are dynamic even in adults, as experiences and behaviour of ourselves and others, which we consider significant are internalised and repeated or copied later.

Eric Berne had originally represented the ego states by three stacked circles, with Parent at the top, Adult in the middle and Child at the bottom, with the Parent and Child circles divided into Structuring Parent and Nurturing Parent, and Free Child and Adapted Child respectively (see Fig. 1.1).

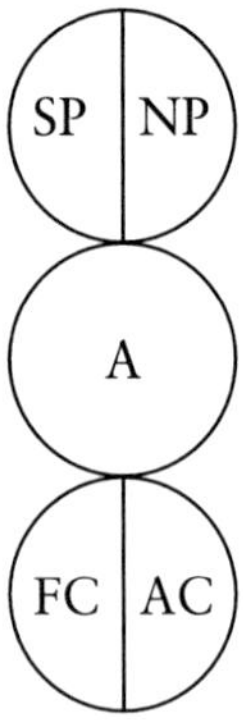

Fig. 1.1: The Ego States

SP = Structuring Parent
NP = Nurturing parent
A = Adult
FC = Free Child
AC = Adapted Child

However, since then, diverse representations of the ego states have been used by various practitioners. They have been represented as parts of a triangle (Holloway, 1977), rectangles within a larger rectangle (Ohlsson, 1988), quadrants (De Luca & Tosi, 2011) and three-dimensional spheres (Baskerville, 2022). However, for our purpose and the sake of simplicity, we will consider the model of **Internal** and **Functional** ego states (Hay, 2009). In this model, the Functional ego states are as given in Fig. 1.2 and represent our observable behaviour as emanating from one or the other ego state, while the Internal ego states are shown next to them as three circles labelled simply Parent, Adult and Child (Fig. 1.2). They were originally dotted to emphasize the fact that they are internal; however, I have shown them as solid circles. The Internal Parent ego state contains internalized copies of all the parents and other authority figures we have known (the smaller circles inside). The Internal Child ego state is represented as being similar to the rings of a tree, with the rings containing our diverse experiences—some good and some bad—while growing up (the smaller circles inside). The Internal Adult ego state receives information (stimulus e.g., someone talking to you) from the external world and decides upon an appropriate response from a particular ego state. All this, naturally, happens much faster than the time I have taken to write it; save in the case of circumstances that I will discuss later.

Behaviour can come from any one of the Functional ego states and be driven by any one of the Internal ego states.

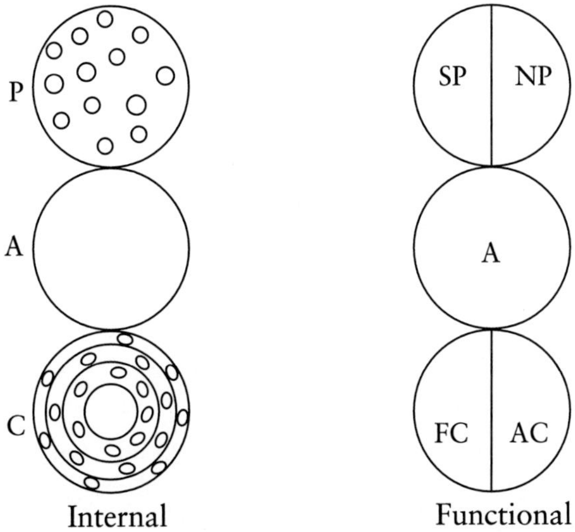

Fig. 1.2: Internal and Functional Ego States

For example:

My colleague and I are both going to work in the morning. As we take the lift to the seventh floor, I ask her,

"What's the time?"

Viewed at one level, this is an Adult to Adult stimulus, a straightforward request for information. However, there may be a tinge of anxiety in my tone about being late. She subconsciously picks up on this and says soothingly,

"Don't worry, we are well in time".

Maybe when she was a child and waiting for the school bus, her mother had told her comfortingly, "Don't worry dear, we have plenty of time".

In this case, her Internal Parent replays this and she answers from her Nurturing Parent.

Or maybe she had a quarrel with her spouse before leaving for work and is in a bad mood. When she was a child and they had gone to a toy store, her father had asked her to pick out a doll, she had pointed to a racing car and said, "I want that", whereupon her father had said exasperatedly, "Why don't you take a doll like every other little girl?"

In this case, she snaps at me, "Why can't you wear a watch like everyone else?"

Her Internal Parent is driving the Structuring Parent response.

Or she might say anxiously, "We will hopefully be well in time". This is her Internal Child expressing itself through Adapted Child behaviour.

Or she might say, "So what, who cares around here?" A Free Child response driven by a rebellious experience that is stored in her Internal Child.

Or she might say, "It's ten to nine".

However, it is important to keep in mind that this division into Internal and Functional ego states has been done only for reasons of clarity. In reality, the Internal Parent and the Functional Parent are one and the same, as are the Internal Adult and Functional Adult, and Internal Child and Functional Child.

In TA terms, the Adult gets contaminated when prejudices internalised from our parental and other authority figures of our childhood make their way into our Adult ego state. In this case, we are liable to make prejudiced statements as adults and express opinions as facts. Similar contamination occurs when instinctive or internalised childlike feelings get into the Adult and are expressed as childlike behaviour at inappropriate times. A simple diagram of Contamination is shown in Fig. 1.3. A major task of the TA therapist is to decontaminate the Adult from these influences.

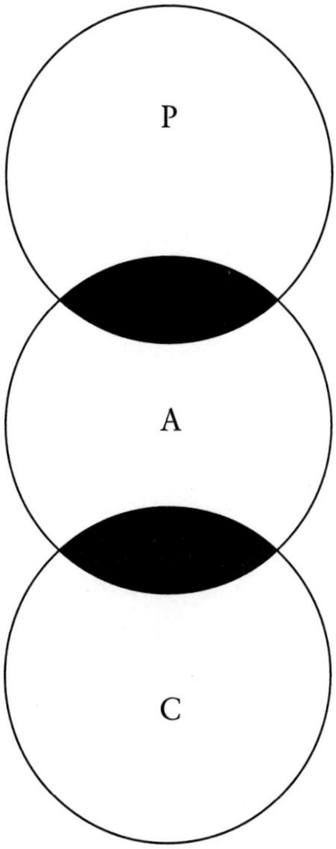

Fig. 1.3: Contamination

For example,

Person A to Person B: "Kids nowadays listen to any old thing! In my time we had real music, which they can't appreciate!"

Person X to Person Y: "No matter how hard you work, no one will appreciate you around here. That's just the way it is".

In a nutshell: TA treats the human personality as being composed of three ego states: Parent, Adult and Child. The question of what, if anything, exists in addition to the ego states, has been discussed by several practitioners and researchers at various times. Berne himself had enclosed Parent, Adult and Child within a larger oval, and had stated that he did not know what was in the space beyond the ego states (James, 1981). The concept of the Spiritual Self or Soul has been named the Inner

Core (James, 1981), the "centre of consciousness" called the "Guru Within" independent of the ego states (Chandran, 2007), described as "I-Am", a circle within another larger circle that contains the ego states (Mellor, 2008), an inner core within the Adult ego state named the Mindful Adult (Zvelc, et al., 2011), the see-er or perceiver separate from the ego states (Sandle, 2019) and located within the Child ego state on the grounds that it is the earliest to be formed (Milnes, 2019).

Insights from *Vedanta*

The ancient Indian philosophical system of *Vedanta* offers a wealth of insights that can enrich our understanding of not just the ego states but the total human personality. Most of the texts on which *Vedanta* is based were composed more than 2,000 years ago. Although they need to be understood in the context of the times in which they were written, there is an air of universality about the body of knowledge and belief that constitutes *Vedanta*; indeed, it is also referred to as a part of *Sanatan Dharma,* which can be translated as Perpetual or Eternal Laws of Life. It is not spoken of as being revealed to anyone in particular but is found in teachings imparted by various sages to their pupils.

However, before proceeding further, I wish to make it clear that I hold no brief for any particular religion. My concern is with spirituality, the belief (or conviction, if you will) that we are a part of something greater than ourselves, and our lives have a definite meaning and purpose. I will use "God" and "Supreme Principle" interchangeably to describe that which is greater than ourselves for the sake of readers who may take exception to the former word "God".

Vedanta means the culmination or essence of the *Vedas*, which are Indian religious texts probably written down around 1500–1000 BCE (although, as an oral tradition, they are probably much older). The spiritual philosophy of the *Vedas* is elaborated in the *Upanishads* (c. 1000–600 BCE), discourses given by various sages to their pupils, and in the *Bhagavad Gita* (c. 900 BCE), a dialogue between *Krishna*, the manifestation of the Supreme Principle, and the warrior, *Arjuna*.

The *Taittiriya Upanishad* describes the total human personality as being composed of five concentric sheaths surrounding an inner core. Over several verses, the sage explains the nature of the *Pancha Kosha* (five sheaths). The outermost is called the *Annamaya Kosha* or **Food Sheath,** which is the physical body, including the five senses. It is caused by food, maintained by food and finally ends up as food. In other words, the body grows and is sustained through its intake of nutrition, and when it finally perishes, it decays to form food for other living creatures.

Within the *Annamaya Kosha* is the *Pranamaya Kosha* or **Vital Air Sheath,** which consists of the faculties *(Pranas)* directly related to breathing; perception through the sense organs; excretion; digestion; and circulation (of nutrition through the bloodstream).

Inside the *Pranamaya Kosha* is the *Manomaya Kosha*, the **Sheath of Mental Impressions,** which is filled with data from the five senses. It is also the repository of passions and emotions, feelings and impulses, likes and dislikes. It controls the two outer sheaths, for example, when the mind is disturbed, the physiological functions *(pranas)* and the physical body are affected.

Within the Sheath of Mental Impressions lies the *Vijnanamaya Kosha*, the **Sheath of Discriminating Intellect.** It is the sheath of directed or guided mental activity, and functions as discriminating, reasoning, reflecting, thinking and analysing. It controls the outer three sheaths.

The innermost sheath is the *Anandamaya Kosha* or **Bliss Sheath,** which we as ordinary human beings achieve when we are in deep dreamless sleep. In this state, we experience bliss in the sense of being undisturbed and completely at peace. The sage explains the Bliss Sheath by saying that the true nature of man is *Ananda* (bliss) and it is only ignorance that draws a veil over that bliss and creates misery in us.

We note that only the outermost sheath is made of matter as we know it, and the others are energy states invisible to the physical eye, though we can sense their presence inside us when we pay close attention.

The five sheaths or the fivefold sheath encircle an inner core called the *Atman* or **Self.** It is this Self that gives life to the body, mind and intellect. In other words, it is the life-principle within us that enables our body to act and perceive, our mind to feel and think, and our intellect to reason. Without it, none of the *Koshas* can function. A simplistic analogy would be electricity and the electric bulb.

The diagrammatic representation of the *Pancha Kosha* model is given in Fig. 1.4 (Swami Parthasarathy, 2000).

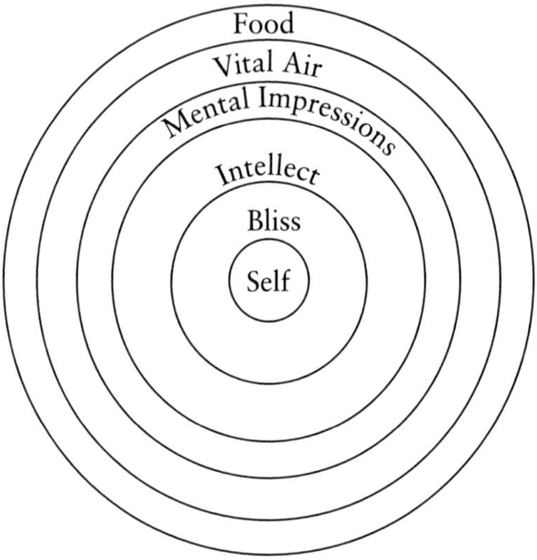

Fig. 1.4: *Pancha Kosha* Model

The discipline of *Yoga* prescribes methods for strengthening the five sheaths. Thus, the *Annamaya Kosha* is strengthened by *Hatha yoga*, a series of exercises and postures (*Asanas*) designed to improve flexibility and mobility. *Pranamaya Kosha* is strengthened through breathing exercises called *Pranayama*, which lead to increased breathing capacity, improved circulation and increased resistance to disease. For strengthening the *Manomaya Kosha*, *Pratyahara* or sensory withdrawal leading to meditation is prescribed, which is said to soothe and balance the flow of mental energy, reduce tension and bring about calmness and tranquillity.

"*Vijnana*" means the power of discernment, discrimination and judgment. The *Vijnanamaya Kosha* is what distinguishes human beings from animals. Although translated as Intellect Sheath, it encompasses the higher functions of the mind, including morality, ethics and will. Mental activity directed by the Intellect Sheath is a uniquely human attribute, and strengthening it is considered to be of prime importance in Yoga. This is done through observance of *Yama* (Vow) and *Niyama* (Rule of Conduct). *Yama* comprises vows of nonviolence, truthfulness, nonstealing, sexual restraint and noncovetousness. The rules of conduct to be followed (*Niyama*) are purity, (both external and internal), contentment, restraint of the senses and meditation, self-study, and surrender to the Supreme Principle.

The *Anandamaya Kosha* or Bliss Sheath is the final sheath between our ordinary awareness and our higher Self. Properly speaking, it is not a sheath at all, but rather a reflection of the *Atman*. In the *Anandamaya Kosha*, the *Atman* experiences eternal bliss, a state of perfect peace and contentment, free from all cares. Such a state is realized in deep sleep in the normal course. It is strengthened by *Seva*, selfless service to others, which leads us to identify our innate unity with other human beings; *Bhakti* Yoga or the yoga of devotion to God; and *Samadhi*, intensely focused meditation, which reveals the divine nature of the *Atman*.

A table of the five sheaths: their explanation and the methods of strengthening them are given below (Table 1.1):

Table 1.1: The Fivefold Sheath

S. No.	Sheath	Composition	Nature	Strengthened by
1.	Food	Matter	Physical Body	Hatha Yoga (physical exercise, postures)
2.	Vital Air	Matter/ Energy	Physiological functions connected with breathing. Controls Food Sheath	Pranayama (breathing exercises)

S. No.	Sheath	Composition	Nature	Strengthened by
3.	Mental Impressions	Energy	Sensory data, passions and emotions, feelings and impulses, likes and dislikes. Controls Vital Air Sheath	Pratyahara (withdrawal of senses), meditation
4.	Intellect	Energy	Discriminating, reflecting, analysing, thinking. Controls Mental Impressions Sheath	Observance of Yama (vows of nonviolence, truthfulness, nonstealing, sexual restraint, non-covetousness) and Niyama (rules of purity in body and mind, contentment, restraint of the senses, meditation, self-study including the study of inner self, surrender to the Supreme Principle)
5.	Bliss	Energy (reflection of Atman)	Love, peace, contentment	Selfless service to others, devotion to God, intensely focused meditation

Since we are discussing the personality, I will not dwell further on the Food Sheath and Vital Air Sheath, although they too are of great importance as far as the composite human being is concerned. However, as far as the integration of TA and *Vedanta* is concerned, I will focus in the first instance on the Mental Impressions Sheath and the Intellect Sheath, for it is there that most of the mental activity that TA concerns itself with takes place. It is also there that we can learn how to get rid of our self-limiting beliefs and grow to truly discover ourselves.

2
The Power of the Intellect

"If humanity could think straight, all our strife would disappear. Be it financial or marital, social or national, religious or spiritual".

—Janki Santoke, Vedantic Scholar, 2019.

When we are adults we carry around memories of the authority figures that made an impact on us when we were growing up and memories of the child we were. Of course, these memories keep getting added to, in the sense that we continue to internalize Parental and Childlike behaviour in other people, which we want to emulate. However, in the real physical sense, when we are grown, the Adult is all there is, and the rest are just memories (mental impressions), whether conscious, subconscious or unconscious. To put it another way: as grown-ups we are living, breathing, functioning adults, behaving generally as directed by our Adult ego state, which is normally the decision-maker of our personality. However, TA has been generally focusing more on the Parent and Child ego states, perhaps because TA is born of psychotherapy, and very often psychological problems in adults stem from the Parent and Child ego states. Since my objective is self-development and personal growth of individuals, I believe it is important to examine the role of the Adult ego state in more detail.

TA and the Adult

The Adult ego state was originally considered to be akin to a computer, concerned with analysis, reasoning, computing and the like. It was also the ego state in contact with the here and now, that is, the external environment and the present time (current reality). It is "concerned with the autonomous processing of data (*from the senses*) and estimating probabilities to decide the future course of action" (Berne, 1966; words in italics added). However, Dr. Berne later introduced the concept of the Integrated Adult, wherein he hypothesised that the Adult can integrate desirable qualities from the Parent and Child ego states, thereby introducing feelings also (Berne, 1968).

Subsequently, it was proposed that the Adult ego state is located within a loosely rectangular "Mandala" shape, with the Nurturing Parent, Structuring Parent, Adapted Child and Natural Child at the four corners within it. In this model, there are multiple Adult ego states, which can manifest themselves near any one of the four corners, depending on the influence of any of the other ego states on the Adult (Ohlsson, 1988).

A new dimension of the Adult was added when it was proposed that the Adult be divided into two parts: the Photographic Adult, dealing with clarity of perception, attentive listening and noninterpretive recall; and the Combining Adult, which is about exploring alternatives and resolving conflicts (Drego, 2000).

However, a different division was made later: the Reflective Adult and the Creative Adult (Oller-Vallejo, 2002). The same author also proposed the concept of integrating the Adult as a means whereby the personality integrates previously dysfunctional parts of the Parent and Child into the Adult (Oller-Vallejo, 2003).

Dr. Berne's early idea of Integrated Adult was expanded into the Integrating Adult, which was taken to mean "*processing and integrating feelings, attitudes, thoughts and behaviours appropriate to the here-and-now at all ages from conception to death*" and to emphasise that such integration is a continuous ongoing process (Tudor, 2003).

In yet another representation of ego states, it was proposed that the Adult has four ego states within it; the Rebellious Adult, the Critical Adult, the Free Adult and the Protective Adult, which were named Developmental Ego States (De Luca & Tosi, 2011).

Very recently, it has been suggested that the Adult itself develops with the passage of time, with different "life tasks" to be performed at different stages of life. Beyond adolescence, five stages have been demarcated as Emerging Adult, Early Adult, Middle Adult, Mature Adult and Late Adult, shown as concentric circles around the core of the Infant, and the circles of the Child and the Adolescent (Cook, 2023). It is recognised that not all psychological problems stem from disturbed Parent or Child ego states but also from conflicts and unresolved tensions associated with the five Adult stages.

> *Development of personality and a sense of self does not end as the adolescent emerges into adulthood...neural pathways continue to grow and change throughout life... adult development (is) in an expanding and dynamic Integrating Adult ego state (Cook, 2023; word in brackets added).*

From the above discussion, it may be seen that there are two common themes that are generally accepted in the TA community. The first is that the concept of the Adult ego state has evolved from the original one of an emotionless computer to an entity with feelings and even intuition, which undergoes growth and development all through life. The second is that the Adult is concerned more with dealing with the here-and-now reality and its associated problems as compared to dealing with the inner world.

We have already briefly mentioned the spiritual dimension of TA that TA researchers have been in search of: the "Inner Core" (James, 1981), and "Guru Within" as a sort of seat of wisdom and universal values, which has a conceptual link to the Integrated Adult, in that the Guru Within "is a repository of the past operating in the present and guided by universal values" (Chandran, 2007). Subsequently, in another development, Mindfulness-Based Transactional Analysis (MBTA) workshops were conceptualised and conducted by a TA practitioner to promote the wellbeing of the participants (Zvelc, et al.,

2011). They define mindfulness as "*nonjudgmental, accepting awareness of one's own experience in the current moment. Such awareness can include internal experiences (thoughts, feelings and physical sensations) and/or external stimuli (e.g., sounds, colours, odours) that an individual becomes aware of in an allowing manner, without trying to suppress them*". The key themes in mindfulness are awareness (of what is happening around you) and acceptance (of the same). The same author regards mindfulness to be at the heart of the integrating process in the Integrating Adult ego state, and represents it diagrammatically as a smaller circle within the Adult ego state with arrows reaching out into the external world and shorter arrows reaching into the inner ego states (Zvelc, 2010, Fig. 4). He considers the Adult to have two main modes of functioning: doing (i.e., responding to external stimuli and problem-solving) and being (acceptance of the present moment, i.e., mindfulness). A characteristic of mindfulness is "bcing witness to our own experience" (Zvelc, 2011), and the MBTA programme is meant to promote understanding and dealing with our negative thoughts, feelings and behaviour.

Vedanta and the Adult Ego State

In the *Pancha Kosha* model, it is evident that the Adult ego state is spread over the Mental Impressions Sheath and the Intellect Sheath. In fact, the Parent and Child ego states, being only memories, also belong to the Mental Impressions Sheath. So if I were to represent the ego states superimposed over the *Pancha Kosha* model, the result would be as in Fig. 2.1.

Now, we have seen that the Intellect Sheath is considered to be distinctly separate from the Mental Impressions Sheath and also as controlling it. This distinction is highlighted in a famous verse from the *Katha Upanishad* (trans. Easwaran, 1981):

> "*Know the Self as Lord of the chariot,*
> *The body as the chariot itself,*
> *The discriminating intellect as the charioteer;*
> *The mind as the reins;*
> *The senses, say the wise, are the horses,*
> *Selfish desires are the roads they travel*".

This analogy, through its visual impact, shows how easy it is to be led astray by the horses (senses) were it not for the guidance of the charioteer—the intellect. Just as the horses want to go astray were it not for the reins (mind) that keep them aligned, our senses can lead us astray were it not for the mind that keeps them aligned. But the reins are nothing without the sobering guidance of the charioteer (intellect) that controls them. In *Vedanta* then, the intellect is treated as entirely separate from, and controlling, the mind. Therefore, Fig. 2.2 shows a smaller circle within the Adult that represents the Intellect Sheath. The Parent and Child ego states are in the Mental Impressions Sheath, while the Adult occupies the Intellect Sheath and part of the Mental Impressions Sheath. Recalling the functions of the Intellect Sheath according to *Vedanta*—discriminating, analysing, reasoning, reflecting, judgement, decision, rectitude—*it can be distinguished as an entirely separate system within the Adult ego state*. The functioning of the Intellect Sheath bears a close correspondence to the structural properties of the Adult ego state, giving rise to the hypothesis that *the Discriminating Intellect Sheath operates on the Sheath of Mental Impressions, which is the repository of all our subjective experience, to choose and decide how we will think, feel and act*. In doing so, however, it is guided by considerations of morality, ethics and will, since it is home to these higher qualities also. In this respect, the Intellect Sheath is similar to the concept of the "Guru Within" in the paper of Sashi Chandran referred to earlier.

If we keep in mind Eric Berne's insistence that one should not say anything that one cannot draw, it is required to diagram the workings of the Adult ego state in terms of the *Pancha Kosha* model. Such a diagram would be as shown in Fig. 2.1, which I have named the **Vedantic Ego States Model.**

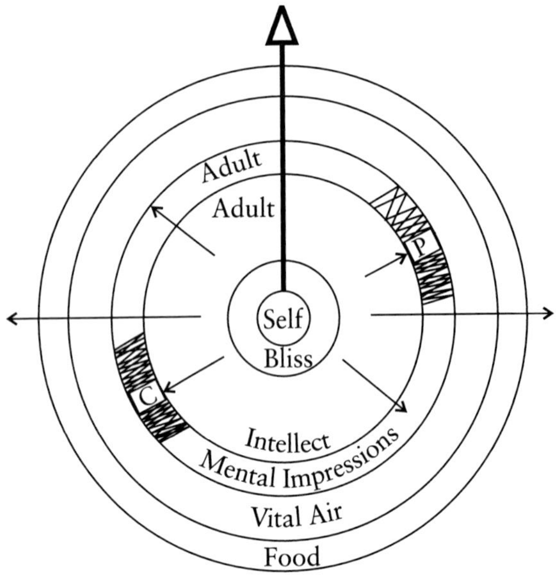

Fig. 2.1: Vedantic Ego States Model

P = Parent
C = Child

The arrows from the Intellect Sheath reaching outside the fivefold sheath represent the engagement of the intellect with external reality as perceived through our senses. The arrows reaching into that part of the Adult contained in the Mental Impressions Sheath show its operation on the mental impressions contained in the Adult ego state, whereas the arrows into the shaded Parent and Child ego states represent its selection of the impressions contained in them, as it judges appropriate. The solid vertical arrow from the *Atman* (also translated as "Self" and what we generally understand as "Soul") reaching upwards represents the longing for *Moksha* in *Vedanta* and Physis/aspiration arrow in TA, which we will discuss in more detail later.

It needs to be mentioned that *Vedanta* distinguishes between two types of knowledge: lower knowledge and higher knowledge. Lower knowledge can broadly be equated with information and its processing, whereas higher knowledge refers to the wisdom absorbed through study and reflection upon the information. It is logical to place lower knowledge (the Adult impressions of external reality) in that part of the Mental Impressions Sheath and higher knowledge in the Intellect Sheath.

Nature of the Intellect Sheath

The *Bhagavad Gita* (Song of the Lord) from the epic poem *Mahabharata* gives an overview of the functioning of the Intellect Sheath as discriminating between opposites: reflecting, analysing, reasoning and judgment, in the sense of judging the correct course of action:

"*Buddhi (Intellect) has three main functions; discrimination, judgement and decision*" (Swami Rama, 1996).

Discrimination: *Vedanta* teaches us that there are two classes of things that the mind gets attracted to: *Preyas*, that which is pleasant in the short term, and *Shreyas*, that which is good, capable of bringing about lasting happiness:

> "*The good and the pleasant approach a man; the wise man considers and distinguishes between the two. Wisely does he prefer the good to the pleasant; but a fool chooses the pleasant for its worldly good [benefit]*". (Katha Upanishad II, 1.2 and 3 trans. Paramahamsa Yogananda)

The discriminating power of the Intellect Sheath makes us aware of the difference between *Shreyas* and *Preyas* (the good and the pleasant). Since it is also the repository of the higher qualities of morality, ethics and character, it points our actions in the direction of *Shreyas*. As an illustration, consider an example from everyday life:

I am travelling in a car and drinking water from a mineral water bottle. When I finish the bottle, I have a fleeting urge to roll down the window and throw it out on the road. I will get the satisfaction of having cleared the car of clutter. However, if I have a sense of responsibility towards the environment, I will wait until pulling up in an area where there is a trash bin, and dispose of it there. My action has been guided by the choice of Shreyas over Preyas.

The above is a mundane example, but a little reflection on the part of the reader will reveal plenty of more serious choices in life, where we could be (and frequently are) guided by the discriminating intellect into choosing long-term good over short-term pleasure, and act accordingly.

Judgement and Decision: The Intellect Sheath receives, perceives and reflects upon information from the first three sheaths. The act of perception is important since, at any given time, there are myriad sensations bombarding our senses. Thus, one may hear birds chirping outside the window, the noise of traffic on the road, music playing on the radio, smell the coffee being brewed, see a painting on the wall, and so on, all at the same time. All these are received in the Sheath of Mental Impressions. However, we will focus on only the stimuli the intellect wants us to focus on, to the exclusion of all else, and respond accordingly.

The judgement and decision functions, ideally speaking, are guided by the values that are inherently a part of the Intellect Sheath such as ethics, morality, sense of responsibility and integrity.

The Intellect Sheath is also home to *Purushartha,* which can be translated as the meaning or objective of life. These are four in number as follows (Chakraborty, 1995):

- *Dharma*, living a life of ethical and moral responsibility.

  (In fact, this Sanskrit word has a whole spectrum of meanings, encompassing morals, ethics, responsibility, obligations, individual duty, law of life and consciousness of the self-aware universe. However, in the context of *Purushartha,* the meaning is as given above.)
- *Artha*, lawful acquisition of wealth.
- *Kama*, enjoyment of the pleasures of the senses.
- *Moksha*, liberation or attaining a state of spiritual perfection. According to Vedantic tradition, these objectives are to be fulfilled in a mutually balanced manner, that is, they should not be regarded as independent or mutually exclusive.

We shall examine *Purushartha* in more detail later.

Autonomy and the Integrating Adult

At this stage, it is important to discuss another concept of TA called **autonomy**. It is seen as the objective of learning and applying TA to help ourselves and others make decisions and behave in a manner that is independent of subconscious impulses, which were programmed into us when we were growing up. The attainment of autonomy was originally considered to be manifested by the release or recovery of three capacities: **awareness, spontaneity** and **intimacy** (Berne, 1964). Capacities added later are **responsibility** (Bonds-White and van Beekum, 1995) and **integrity** (Mellor, 2008). Awareness refers to the capacity (ability) to be totally present in the here-and-now, spontaneity to the ability to choose between a range of options (ego states) to express behaviour and intimacy to the ability to maintain a close relationship with another person. In other words, autonomy comes about when we are fully aware of and dealing with the present situation and environment, as opposed to responding by way of conditioned behaviour; when we are able to make a considered choice of the most appropriate behaviour from a range of options; when we are genuinely open, honest and authentic with each other (Berne, 1964); when we take full responsibility for our actions and believe that we are responsible for ourselves alone and no one else; and when we are able to discover meaning in our life experiences to live honestly and in accordance with our principles.

However, it has also been shown through a research project that autonomy can be summarized in two variables: contact with self and contact with others (Van Beekum, 2000). Contact with self includes access to internal dialogue (e.g., between ego states), taking action and taking a stand based on own thoughts whereas contact with others relates to attitudes formed while interacting with others like encouraging, discounting, open minded, prejudiced, etc. To that extent, real autonomy may only come about when we move between contact with ourselves and contact with another.

The optimal state of autonomy is one in which certain desirable qualities of Parent and Child ego states are integrated into the Adult ego state (Berne, 1968), as mentioned earlier. As we have seen, it is currently emphasised that integration is an ongoing process (Tudor, 2003); therefore, the Adult ego state is in a state of continuous development process and is by no means a static entity. It is characterised by emotional, cognitive and moral development, creativity, and the capacity for full engagement in meaningful relationships.

In relation to *Vedanta*, we may postulate that the progress towards autonomous functioning of the Adult ego state *is due to strengthening and enabling the Intellect Sheath as it operates on the Mental Impressions Sheath with increasing effectiveness* to determine how we think, feel and act, using as its yardsticks *Shreyas* and *Dharma*. To probe more deeply into its functioning, consider the stated components of autonomy—awareness, spontaneity, intimacy, responsibility and integrity—in the light of the Vedantic Ego States Model.

Awareness: Here and Now *and* There and Then

The model presented by Zvelc, et al. (2011) of the Mindful Adult (Zvelc, 2011) shows the Adult ego state with a central core of the Mindful Adult, and, in this respect, it is similar to the Vedantic Model. Surely, the Intellect Sheath possesses the quality of mindfulness, which is defined as the ability to focus on the here and now in a nonjudgmental and accepting manner. However, the Intellect Sheath also possesses the ability to detach us from the current reality and focus our attention on something far removed from our present circumstances, when it is in our best interest to do so. As an extreme example, consider the case of Dr. Viktor Frankl, who was able to survive horrific brutalities in the Nazi concentration camp by deliberately detaching his mind from the here and now, and imagining that he was talking to his wife:

> *"In front of me a man stumbled and those following him fell on top of him. The guard rushed over and used his whip on them all... But soon my soul found*

its way back from the prisoner's existence to another world and I resumed talk with my loved one..."

—Viktor E. Frankl, Man's Search for Meaning, 1959

At other times, Viktor E. Frankl would imagine himself giving a lecture on psychology in a warm and comfortable lecture hall (quoted from his book: *Man's Search for Meaning*):

> *"I limped a few kilometres with our long column of men from the camp to our work site. Very cold, bitter winds struck us. I kept thinking of the endless little problems of our miserable life... Suddenly I saw myself standing on the platform of a well-lit, warm and pleasant lecture room. In front of me sat an attentive audience on comfortable upholstered seats. I was giving a lecture on the psychology of the concentration camp!..."*

Clearly, he was able to preserve his sanity, and possibly even his life, by detaching his mind from the current reality. Or consider an example from everyday life:

Let us say we have to receive an injection. It is common practice to look away from the spot where the injection is to be administered, and think of something else; by doing so, we hardly feel the painful prick of the needle.

Therefore, it is evident that the intellect has the power to make us detach from the external world and focus on the internal world. It is as if the Intellect Sheath acts as a regulator, capable not only of switching on and switching off internal and external worlds, but also of controlling how much of both engage our attention at any given moment, and of moving back and forth between the two. To that extent, the intellect, then, in addition to the quality of mindfulness, also possesses the power to detach the mind from the immediate environment and acts as an internal regulator (charioteer), controlling in our own interest, how much of the internal and external worlds engage our attention at any given time. This also fits in with the research finding that real autonomy may only come about when we move between contact with ourselves and contact with another (van Beekum, 2000), with the proviso that it is the strengthened Intellect Sheath that regulates this contact.

Spontaneity

In the light of the arrows reaching into the mental impressions residing in the Parent and Child ego states in the Vedantic model, it can be appreciated how the Intellect Sheath picks up what it considers desirable from them according to its judgement and decision functions, and reproduces or exhibits the corresponding behaviour appropriately. In fact, spontaneity is closely tied to the judgement function of the Intellect Sheath. It rapidly assesses the environment and the situation, decides an appropriate behavioural response, selects from among a range of options and picks the one most suited to the situation. However, this process is not automatic, as in the case of a computer algorithm, although much of the time it may be lightning fast. At other times, it may well be slower and more deliberate because it is *deliberated* by the intellect, the reasoning, reflecting and analysing part of our consciousness.

Responsibility and Integrity

Shreyas and *Dharma* are two of the guiding criteria for the Intellect Sheath to make the Adult ego state behave responsibly. In the example of the mineral water bottle referred to earlier, the intellect makes use of *Shreyas* to determine my actions. If I am conscious of the long-term consequences of my actions, I will take steps to see that they do not degrade the environment. *Dharma,* however, is more complex. For the moment, I will suggest that the Intellect Sheath, ideally speaking, has the decisive say in working out my personal *Dharma,* that is, my rightful duty as a person. In this way, I am actually taking a step further down the road to autonomy by examining and critically evaluating old ideas in my Mental Impressions Sheath/Parent and Child, in terms of their relevance to the present time or my present situation. Therefore, the intellect is the agency which, ideally speaking, decides my moral and ethical code (*Dharma*). If it doesn't perform this function, then it means that the intellect is not that strong in me, and I am prone to slavishly follow the dictates of my (subconscious) Parent and Child. On the other hand, if the Intellect Sheath is strong, it guides me to formulate my *Dharma,* which may be influenced by the contents of my Parent and Child, but is finally decided by my own analysis, reflection and judgement.

Integrity means consistency of words and action, thought and deed, as well as the quality of being honest, and having strong moral principles and ethical values. In this connection, observance of *Yama* and *Niyama,* prescribed for strengthening the Intellect Sheath, is relevant insofar as living a life of responsibility and integrity is concerned (Ref. Table 1.1). *Vedanta* also lays great stress on doing one's rightful duty, that is, being true to oneself or acting with absolute integrity; the entire *Bhagavad Gita* is an exhortation to the central character of the *Mahabharata,* Arjuna, to follow his *Dharma.*

It will be appropriate to discuss Intimacy subsequently, since according to *Vedanta,* it is not considered to be a part of the *Pancha Kosha* at all.

The Cultural Parent and the Intellect Sheath: Working Out One's *Dharma*

At this stage, I would like to introduce the TA concept of the **Cultural Parent** (Drego, 1983). This will be helpful in delving deeper into the working of the Intellect Sheath. Briefly speaking, every person carries around in his head the belief system, behavioural cues and range of feelings (named respectively, etiquette, technicalities and character) internalised by him from the culture that he grew up in. It is formed in the family and the sociocultural environment the child grows up in, and the appropriate place for this set of rigid beliefs, behaviour and feelings is in the Parent ego state. It is shown as three ellipses within the Parent ego state (Fig. 2.2).

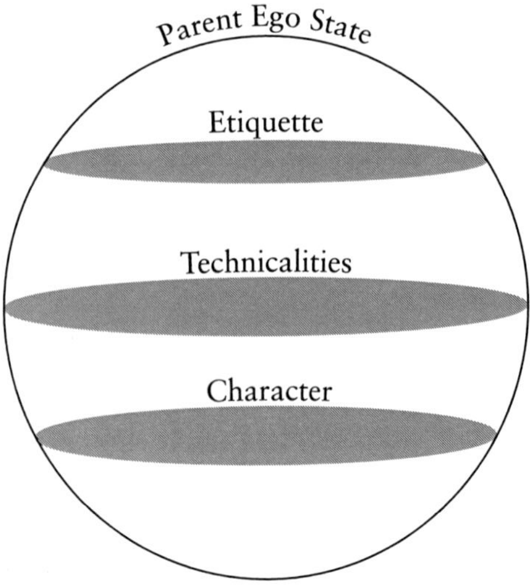

Fig. 2.2: The Cultural Parent

Drego explains "*An unhealthy Cultural Parent is one which wants to (1) repeat old history over and over again without change; (2) keep things the way they are, because this is safe and familiar; (3) assume responsibility for others that these others can well assume for themselves; (4) provide punishments for new and untried behaviour even where such behaviour is life-giving and healthy; (5) keep power over others and enjoy controlling them for the sake of controlling; (6) destroy anything, however good, that threatens the maintenance of control*".

The Intellect Sheath provides a powerful weapon with which to suppress the unhealthy Cultural Parent (on an individual level), if only we will let it. We all possess the power to work out our individual *Dharma,* or rightful duties and responsibilities.

The earliest influence that shaped my *Dharma* is my cultural background. As a child, my parents and other authority figures of my childhood taught me what was right and what was wrong. However, this is contained in the Cultural Parent part of my Parent, which in turn is contained in my Mental Impressions Sheath. This is however subordinate to the Intellect Sheath. It is actually the discriminating intellect—the moral, ethical, thinking, reflecting, analysing and reasoning part of the mind, as shown in Fig. 2.1—which should ideally decide our behaviour and actions. Examples of a person's *Dharma* may be the proper discharge of their professional or familial roles, for example, doctor, teacher, parent, etc. It is important to note that *Dharma* is a flexible concept and can also embrace a combination of things. Different stages of life may call for different *Dharmas* or rightful purposes (For example, a professional may need to transition to the role of a parent and then later back to being a professional). Therefore, my *Dharma,* then, ideally should be what makes sense to me as my duty at that time, within the framework of my moral and ethical responsibilities. This is decided by the Intellect Sheath (charioteer).

I will consider an example each of etiquette, technicalities and character of the Cultural Parent to show how these can be (and indeed are) overcome by the Intellect Sheath.

Etiquette

In India, not too long ago, it was unthinkable to marry outside one's caste or community; the Cultural Parent etiquette strongly forbade such an aberration. However, in modern times, intercaste and intercommunity marriages are becoming increasingly common in India, among the urban elite in the cities, and are accepted by both families. The people concerned have overcome the traditional way of thinking imposed earlier and have concluded that such barriers are no longer relevant in today's context.

Technicalities

An integral part of Hindu households is a Mandir, a place for worship, even if it is a simple shelf on the wall. It is usually adorned with idols and pictures of various gods, goddesses and saints. The technicality of Cultural Parent tradition dictates the lighting of incense sticks there at the time of worship. However, in the cities, many people stay in high-rise apartments, where such smouldering sticks could pose a fire hazard. My Intellect Sheath could very well recognize the hazard and override my Cultural Parent so that I worship without lighting incense. If I am uncomfortable in not doing so (after all, Cultural

Parent traditions are hard to break), my Intellect Sheath could alternatively reach a compromise whereby I perform my worship, and then extinguish the incense stick, thus satisfying both requirements of tradition and safety requirements in the modern context.

Character

The routine bodily function of menstruation used to be culturally associated with uncleanliness in many places including India. Traditionally, women belonging to higher caste Indian families were not permitted to enter their kitchens, and in some cases, their homes also, when they were having their periods, on the grounds of being unclean. This unwarranted oppression naturally resulted in a feeling of guilt and shame on the part of the woman concerned, as if it was somehow her fault. But the times are changing, and the intellect is now strong enough to override such wholly unnecessary feelings; the modern Indian woman and her family members think nothing of her entering the kitchen or any other place at that time of the month.

Effectively Using the Intellect Sheath

We have already seen that *Vedanta* prescribes methods for developing the powers of the intellect (observance of *Yama* and *Niyama*, ref. Table 1.1). In addition to these, there are simple routines that can be followed on an everyday basis for the same purpose. Some of these are described below:

Isolation: We can set aside a specific time of the day (preferably early in the morning) to be alone, and spend this time in silence and contemplation. It does not matter what we contemplate, as long as we focus on ourselves and our thoughts. We can try to cultivate the practice of observing our thoughts dispassionately, neither judging nor criticising ourselves but just being aware of them. In terms of visualisation, it would be akin to sitting silently and watching a movie of our thoughts.

Introspection: Just before going to bed, we can spend some time introspecting. This involves recollection of our activities on that day, from the time of getting out of bed to the time we do this. In the beginning, it may be difficult to recollect all our activities. Once again, we observe dispassionately, neither judging nor criticising, but this time we make a mental note of the times we have acted unthinkingly or impulsively. The idea is to estimate, over the course of the day, how many times the intellect has not been available to us. If we practise introspection regularly, the intellect can be strengthened so that it comes into play most of the time, and guides our actions and behaviour accordingly.

We note that in TA terms the Integrating Adult incorporates positive feelings (emotions) from the Child and positive structuring (morality, ethics and sense of responsibility) from the Parent. The Intellect Sheath is therefore a composite of these qualities, and our introspection is not merely an intellectual exercise but rather a dispassionate analysis of the occasions on which we did not make use of our Integrating Adult.

Self-Study and Reflection: Again, we need to set aside a specific time of the day for gaining knowledge. It is particularly recommended to study the works of the noted philosophers, mystics and poets, and the lives of great men. Each distinct period of reading should be followed by a spell of reflection *(manan)*, for this is the way knowledge is converted into wisdom. The methods for reflection include: questioning (what has been read); logical and lateral thinking; recognizing and analysing other perspectives; deducing, inducing and synthesizing. We will consider such methods in more detail later.

As mentioned earlier, we associate lower knowledge with the part of the Adult contained in the Mental Impressions Sheath, with higher knowledge belonging to the Intellect Sheath. Reflection leads us to a higher knowledge of concepts, values, responsibility (*dharma*), morality and ethics.

We note that developing the Intellect Sheath and using it effectively provides a method to override the unhealthy parts of our Cultural Parent and also a way to analyse, discriminate, reason logically, plan and forecast. This is in addition to its power to choose the correct response in any given situation, as we have seen. Since it is also the home of our sense of ethics, morality and responsibility, the comparison to the "charioteer" of the composite human personality is particularly appropriate.

(In the Mahabharata, putting Lord Krishna, the manifestation of the Supreme Principle, in the role of charioteer to the warrior Arjuna, seems to be deliberately done, consistent with the analogy in the Katha Upanishad quoted earlier.)

But there is something more beyond the Intellect Sheath, which not only has a bearing on TA theories, but according to *Vedanta*, is of literally the greatest importance for self-development and personal growth, and leads to spiritual growth. We will now explore this.

3

Beyond the Intellect: Our Natural State

"God has created eternal bliss in the innermost area of man's personality"

—Maharishi Mahesh Yogi, spiritual guru, 1972.

Pancha Kosha: The Bliss Sheath and the Self

We have seen how the Intellect Sheath, when properly trained and strengthened is capable of distilling wisdom from knowledge and directing our actions accordingly. In TA terms and in terms of the Vedantic Ego States Model, the progress towards autonomy is driven by the Intellect Sheath. However, *Vedanta* says that there are limits to the powers of the intellect, and by itself, it is not capable of knowing the Ultimate Truth of life. To understand why, we have to probe the workings of the Bliss Sheath and the nature of the Soul/Self (*Atman*).

As we have seen in Chapter I, the Bliss Sheath is achieved when we are in deep dreamless sleep, in the sense that we are undisturbed and completely at peace. Deep sleep is also the time when the body recharges itself; the conscious mind shuts down and automatic functions take over. We feel completely refreshed after a good night's sleep and miserable mentally and physically when deprived of sleep. Indeed, it is common to use the phrase 'slept like a baby' to describe feeling fresh, healthy and energetic.

Vedanta describes three states of consciousness: waking, dream sleep and deep sleep. It further posits that the Bliss

Sheath is home to the *Vasanas* (inherent desires and urges) of the personality. These inherent urges are however suppressed in the deep sleep state (Bliss Sheath). They manifest as thoughts during dream sleep and result in unthinking or instinctive actions in the waking state. However, the latter can be and are controlled and overridden by the intellect.

As mentioned earlier, the Bliss Sheath itself is a reflection of the Self, which is the Ultimate Truth, our real nature.

But what is this Self?

Vedanta talks about Consciousness as the thread that binds together the three stages of waking, dream sleep and deep sleep. Consciousness is what enables the eye to see, the ear to hear, the nose to smell, the fingers to touch, the tongue to taste and the lungs to draw breath. It also enables the mind to think and the intellect to function. This Consciousness minus the Vasanas or inherent urges is the Self.

Sat Chit Ananda

Further, the Self is described as ***Sat-Chit-Ananda*** or **Existence-Consciousness-Bliss.** (Indeed, Satchidanand is a well-known name among Indians). Let us now probe more deeply into these terms.

The sage asks his pupil,

> *"What is that knowledge by which everything becomes known?"*

—Chhandogya Upanishad, trans. Swami Sarvapriyananda

He explains that the manifestation of anything needs to be traced back to the original source to know its innate nature. For example, if we know clay, we know all pots made of clay are nothing but clay, by knowing iron, we understand all implements made of iron, and if we know gold, we can understand the essence of all things made of gold. This essence is called *Sat*; Existence or (Inmost) Truth. And so, the *Atman* or Self at the core of the human personality is Pure Existence; the personality (including the body) could not be formed without it.

We note in passing that this is very similar to Plato's Theory of Ideas: the idea of a man is the idea Man. Indeed, it is said that Plato, during his travels, reached India and learned from the sages (Durant, 1926). Also, the Vedantic Existence is completely different from the philosophy of Existentialism, which holds that existence precedes essence, and denies ideas and ideals completely. *Vedanta*, on the other hand, upholds the primacy of both.

But there's more.

> *"The disciple asked. By whose will directed does the mind proceed to its object? At whose will do men utter speech? Who is the God that directs the eyes and ears?*
>
> *The teacher replied: It is the Ear of the ear, the Mind of the mind, the Speech of speech, the Life of life, and the Eye of the eye..."*
>
> —*Kena Upanishad, trans. Paramhansa Yogananda*

Let us try to understand this. Our bodies are made of matter—flesh, bone, organs, etc.,—but we have a first-person awareness of our bodies: I am consciously aware of my body. Similarly, I am conscious of the colours in a rainbow, the beauty of a sunset, and the redness of a rose. The vividness of these experiences is undisputed; in Western philosophy, it is called *qualia*, the conscious awareness of a subjective experience. This is not a product of the body or even the mind. Our bodies are made of matter and our minds are energy fields whose constituents are sensory data and the faculties of the intellect. However, such a consciousness is radically different from either. It pervades and illumines the mind and body and enables all mental and sensory functions—thinking, seeing, hearing, feeling, speaking, and so on. It is 'known' only through its manifestations in the various functions of the mind, organs and body. Without the body and mind, as in deep sleep, consciousness cannot be known or experienced—yet, it continues to exist. The *Vedic* sage calls it *Chit* or Pure Consciousness, and locates it in the Self—the core of our being. Since it is pure consciousness unfettered by the limitations of the physical and mental bodies or by logic and reasoning, its very nature makes it difficult to describe in words. It cannot be defined, since to define is to limit, and *Chit* is surely unlimited and it can only be experienced.

Vedanta further states that the natural state of the Self is bliss, which gets hidden because of the activity of the senses, and the mixture of emotions, desires and instincts that make up the human personality. This is however not the same as the bliss experienced in the Bliss Sheath. Recall that in the Vedantic Ego States Model, the Bliss Sheath manifests as undisturbed peace and tranquillity as in deep sleep, when inherent desires and urges are submerged. But the Bliss Sheath is itself a reflection of the Self. If I compare this sheath to a clouded mirror, then the bliss that shines through it is partly obscured by the inherent urges (*vasanas*), submerged though they may be. If I can get rid of these inherent urges, I can penetrate this sheath (clean the mirror) and gain realisation of the Self, I am left with Pure Bliss.

In TA, four primary emotions are recognised: Fear, Anger, Sadness and Happiness, each of which is said to arise in a person in response to a need, for example, fear arises because of the need for security. However, the natural and most fundamental emotional state of a person is thought to be happiness (Koopmans, 2019). In Vedantic terms, however, this is considered to be a reflection of bliss experienced by the Self—*Ananda.*

And so, in the Vedantic tradition, the Self is known as *Sat Chit Ananda* or Pure Existence-Consciousness-Bliss. Indeed, knowledge of the Self is said to be—in addition to the three previously mentioned states of waking, dream sleep and deep sleep—the fourth and ultimate state *(turiya).*

But how to realise this state?

Self-Realisation

Vedanta prescribes four methods:

Karma Yoga, the yoga of action

Jnana Yoga, the yoga of knowledge

Bhakti Yoga, the yoga of devotion

Raja Yoga, the yoga of meditation.

Yoga is a much misunderstood term, colloquially understood to mean a set of bodily exercises and breathing techniques. This is however *Hatha* Yoga or yoga of the body. The original

Sanskrit term "*Yog*" actually means union (literal translation "going into") and refers to the merging of the Self with the Supreme Principle *Brahman.*

Let us briefly understand these terms:

***Karma* Yoga:** The word *Karma* literally means "deeds" or "actions". However, like *Dharma,* it actually has a whole range of meanings, some of which are quite subtle and require reflection (*manan*) to properly appreciate. In the context of *Karma* Yoga, it means "working in the spirit of service to others" without desire for reward for oneself, and with as much attention to the means as the end:

> *"To work properly, therefore, you have first to give up the idea of attachment... hold yourself as a witness and go on working... yet we must do good. The desire to do good is the highest motive power that we have, if we know all the time that it is a privilege to help others... Be thankful that you are allowed the exercise of benevolence and mercy in the world, and thus become pure and perfect"* (*Swami Vivekananda, Vedanta: Voice of Freedom*).

***Jnana* Yoga**: Jnana Yoga, by definition, means knowledge of the union of the Self with the Supreme Principle. How to achieve this? Recall that the Intellect Sheath is strengthened by Introspection, Study and Reflection to gain knowledge and convert it into wisdom. The last stage in this process is meditation (*nididhyasana*), which leads to knowledge of the Absolute Reality—the Self. (Perhaps "knowledge" is not the right word; "experiencing" or "becoming conscious of" may convey the meaning in simpler terms).

Several steps are prescribed in *Vedanta* for this last and most difficult stage. It begins with mindfulness, then gradual withdrawal of the senses from external reality, control of the mind to the point of tranquillity and detachment, strong, (even intense) faith in the Supreme Principle and the desire to reach it, repeated practice, freeing the mind of sense-attachment, and learning to discriminate between the transitory and the eternal.

This leads finally to direct perception (*pratyaksha*) of the Self/ Supreme Principle.

The French philosopher Voltaire (1694–1778) has an interesting parable on the thirst for knowledge that characterises Jnana Yoga:

The Good Brahmin

I was walking along the banks of the Ganges when I met a Brahmin, a pious fellow...who said,

"I wish I had never been born!"

"Why so?" I asked.

"Because" he replied, "I have been studying these last forty years, and I find it has been so much time lost. I still have no idea where I came from, who I really am, or where I am going...I do not know what the soul is, or even if it exists..."

The same day I had a conversation with an old woman, his neighbour.

I asked her if she was ever unhappy for not understanding how her soul was made. She did not even comprehend my question. She had not, even for a brief moment, thought about those subjects with which the good Brahmin so tormented himself...provided she could get some of the holy water of the Ganges for her rituals and prayers, thought herself the happiest of women... I returned to my philosopher, and said to him,

"Are you not ashamed to be this miserable when, not fifty yards from you, there is an old automaton who thinks of nothing and lives contented?"

"You are right" he replied, "I have said to myself a thousand times that I should be happy if I were as ignorant as my old neighbour, and yet it is a happiness that I do not desire".

***Bhakti* Yoga:** This is a "*real, genuine search after the Lord, a search beginning, continuing and ending in love" (Swami Vivekananda)*. This, however, is not for everybody but only a select few. It requires an intense urge to experience the Supreme Principle without any desire for oneself, without any fear or apprehension, and to keep on searching for the ideal love. As a lover thinks only of the beloved, pursues the beloved fearlessly and sees the highest expression of love in the appearance of the beloved, so too does the *Bhakti* Yoga aspirant approach the object of devotion. It is the Yoga of the heart, as opposed to Yoga of the mind; the intellect has no place in it, and the emotion of love reigns supreme.

Followers of *Bhakti* Yoga are usually marked by a childlike simplicity and charm in their unwavering devotion to the Supreme Principle. In India, the land of sages and saints, it is not uncommon to see holy men dancing and singing with gay abandon as part of their worship. Many of them who have attained a high degree of spiritual perfection are known and revered for their warmth, sincerity and affection.

Organisations such as the International Society of Krishna Consciousness (ISKCON) have been instrumental in spreading the practice of Bhakti Yoga internationally through singing bhajans (devotional songs) and chanting in praise of Lord Krishna, who is revered as a manifestation of the Supreme Principle. Recently, on holiday in Florence, a friend was pleasantly surprised to see a group of Italian devotees in ochre robes and saris, singing bhajans and dancing with gay abandon in the middle of a palazzo.

***Raja* Yoga:** This last and most difficult yoga that involves training the mind, overcoming emotions through *Yama* and *Niyama* (Ref. Table 1.1), yogic posture or *asana*, breathing exercises *(pranayama)*, withdrawal of the senses *(pratyahara)*, concentration *(dharana)*, meditation *(dhyana)* and finally superconsciousness *(samadhi)*. It is said to result in total liberation of the human personality. It is usually practised by *yogis* (spiritual seekers) who live in isolation in their quest for spiritual perfection.

"Thus the man who has practised control over himself cannot be acted upon by anything outside. There is no more slavery for him. His mind has become free". (Swami Vivekananda)

A table of the different types of yoga and their significant characteristics is given below:

Table 3.1: Different Types of *Yoga*

S. No.	Type of Yoga	Related to	Procedure	Benefits	Remarks
1.	Hatha Yoga	Food Sheath, Vital Air Sheath	Yogic postures, Breathing Exercises	Healthy body, improved circulation, improved respiratory system, calmness, tranquillity	Can be done by anyone
2.	Karma Yoga	Mental Impressions Sheath, Intellect Sheath	Nonattachment to reward, "witness" to work, service to others, doing good, gratitude	Inner peace, empathy, control over emotions and instincts	Can be done by anyone
3.	Jnana Yoga	Intellect Sheath, Bliss Sheath, Self	Withdrawal of senses, meditation, faith, repeated practice	Realisation of Self	For seekers of spiritual perfection (monks)
4.	Bhakti Yoga	Bliss Sheath, Self	Intense devotion and desire to know God, feeling of love for all, spirit of selfless service	Realisation of Self	For seekers of spiritual perfection (monks and saints)
5.	Raja Yoga	Bliss Sheath, Self	Withdrawal of senses, intense concentration, prolonged meditation	Realisation of Self	For monks, saints and ascetics

Atman

We now look at the inner core of the Self, which the *Pancha Kosha* envelopes, in a little more detail. It may however be appreciated that spiritual seekers, holy men, saints and ascetics spend decades in the search for experiencing Self-realisation (for it is experiential in nature), and we cannot hope to do justice to it in a few pages. It will suffice if we are able to glean a few insights into the characteristics of the Self, in the hope that our search may aid us in the goal of living honourably and well in the present life.

The peerless Swami Vivekananda describes the Self:

> *"We know how, in olden times, in all the ancient scriptures...manifestation of power was thought to be a bright substance having the form of this body, and which remained even after the body fell. Later on, however, we find a higher idea coming—that this bright body did not represent the force. Whatsoever has form...requires something else behind it to move it...that something was called the soul—Atman, in Sanskrit....the Atman...works the mind, and through the mind, the body... this Atman, whatever it be, has neither form nor shape, and that which has neither form nor shape must be omnipresent...Time, space and causation are in the mind. And as this Atman is beyond the mind and formless, it must be beyond time, beyond space, and beyond causation.... it must be infinite ... The infinite cannot be two. If the soul be infinite, there can be only one Soul, and all ideas of various souls—you having one soul, and I having another, and so forth—are not real. The Real Man therefore is one and infinite, the omnipresent Spirit... the Spirit, being beyond cause and effect, not bound by time and space, must therefore be free... Every soul is infinite. Therefore, there is no question of birth and death".*
>
> *—Swami Vivekananda, Vedanta: Voice of Freedom*

Immortality

And so, the Atman, being immortal,does not die when the body perishes, but simply manifests in another body:

> *"The knowing Self is not born. It does not die. It has not sprung from anything; nothing has sprung from it. Birthless, everlasting, immortal and ancient, it is not killed when the body is killed".*
>
> *—Katha Upanishad, trans. Paramahansa Yogananda*

Again,

> *"As a person gives up old and worn out garments and accepts new apparel, similarly the embodied soul giving up old and worn out bodies verily accepts new bodies".*
>
> —*Bhagavad Gita, trans. Swami Prabhupada*

At once, we recognise the transitory nature of our earthly lives and the relative unimportance of our worldly obsessions. If our essence is really permanent and immortal, and when the body dies, it simply goes to another body, then what price our sorrows, hardships, emotional turmoil and psychological problems in this life? This worldview brings equanimity and fortitude to suffer the "slings and arrows", and a realisation that life's problems are but temporary in nature.

There is an echo of this in Plato's famous *Phaedo*; as Socrates prepares for his execution, he tells his sorrowing disciples:

> *"Be of good cheer, Crito, and say that you are burying my body only".*
>
> —*Phaedo by Plato, trans. B. Jowett*

Or as the French philosopher Pierre Teilhard de Chardin (1881–1955) puts it:

> *"We are not human beings having a spiritual experience; we are spiritual beings having a human experience".*
>
> —*Pierre Teilhard de Chardin*

Observer

The Self is a silent witness to our thoughts, feelings and behaviour. It does not judge, criticise or act. We have the gift of free will and the ability to do good or evil, to be active or passive, to work or be idle. Whatever our mind-body complex does, the soul that gives it life remains unmoved and tranquil.

How can I use this knowledge to my advantage in this, my present life? Through the power of **detachment**. For example, if I am angry about something, I possess the ability to step back and observe myself being angry. Is it really me with a contorted face, narrowed eyes, raising my voice and shouting, arms akimbo, with a threatening posture? Am I not above this?

If I become a witness to my own anger, I will cease being angry. I invite the reader to try to use this technique. It does not require any great stretch of the imagination for me to visualise myself, as I would another person; and the perspective it lends has a valuable effect in calming raging passions immediately.

Similarly, in the case of fear or sadness, if we are able to detach ourselves to the extent that we can see ourselves being scared or sorrowful, we may be able to manage these emotions better. (Of course, in the case of danger, fear is an appropriate response since it generates appropriate mechanisms in the body for a fight or flight response; we are discussing detachment in the context of groundless or imaginary fear). In the event of sadness, we may be able to detach sufficiently to call up the appropriate response, for example, from our Nurturing Parent, in TA terms.

Therefore, it becomes easier to handle our emotions if we understand and acknowledge the Vedantic perspective.

There remains one aspect of the Vedantic Ego States Model (Fig. 2.1) that requires to be discussed in more detail, and that is the solid arrow originating from the Self and going upward beyond the *Pancha Kosha*. To do this, we now return to TA and examine the concept of Physis.

Physis Reimagined

Physis, as originally defined by the philosopher Heraclitus (c.600 BCE) meant, "change or growth which comes from the spirit within the person" (Guerrere, 1980). In TA terms, it is conceived of as a life force, a fundamental urge to grow, evolve and improve, present in living organisms (Berne, 1968). At the individual level, its manifestation is the aspiration for change and human transformation (Clarkson, 1992). However, this aspiration is recognized to be deep-seated and primal, beyond the layers of personality formed by the ego states as the individual grows. Physis is seen as a positive life force, a force of nature seeking greater health (Cornell, 2010). It was thought to be arising from the earliest, most undifferentiated Child ego state.

However, in *Vedanta,* it is said that *Atman* pulsates in every cell of your body. It is the vitalising principle inherent in your mind and intellect... the life-principle or God-principle, within you (Parthasarathy, 2000). Evidently, *Vedanta* considers Physis as springing from the *Atman,* the Self or Soul. As such, I have represented Physis as arising from the Self in the Vedantic Ego States Model. All the organs and agencies of action and thought are powered by the Self, without which there would be no existence or consciousness. (The Intellect Sheath, when properly strengthened and trained helps them to grow and develop to their optimum state; it is, after all, a truism that the mind controls the body). Therefore, the solid arrow rising upward from the Self in the Vedantic Ego States Model represents Physis: the urge to grow, develop, become better. This can also be considered to be the same as the aspiration arrow of the script matrix. (A script is a kind of psychological survival plan formed for the most part in early childhood, when the child unconsciously internalises the behaviour that will enable her to win the approval of her parents and other authority figures, and keeps repeating this behaviour later on in life. It has been diagrammatically represented as the child's ego states influenced by those of her parents, with the aspiration to grow and develop as an arrow rising upward from her Child ego state. Readers interested in learning more about scripts can refer to my earlier book).

Thus, the arrow is shown as rising up beyond the *Pancha Kosha* in the same sense that the aspiration arrow is shown as rising up beyond the ego states, the difference being that the source is not the Child ego state. In my model, the Parent, Adult and Child are simply manifestations of an immortal Essence; the Self, which is the source of Physis.

It may be mentioned that among Western philosophers Arthur Schopenhauer (1788–1860) had conceptualized the innate drive of a human being as the will to survive in this world. At a later date, the philosopher Friedrich Nietzsche (1844–1900) declared the primal urge to be a will to power (over others) and a desire to control. The interpretations of Heraclitus and of TA seem to be much nearer the mark and are also borne out by modern science, as we shall see later.

And so, we reach the end of our journey inward, to the very core of the human being. But the most meaningful spiritual aspect of the personality remains to be discussed and forms the subject matter of the following chapter.

4

A Love Supreme

"I was doing time in the Universal Mind
I was feeling fine..."

—Jim Morrison, American singer-songwriter, 1970.

Intimacy

In Chapter II, we discussed the TA concept of autonomy. The objective of learning TA is to live an **autonomous** life, characterised by **awareness, spontaneity, responsibility, integrity** and **intimacy**, free from the compulsions of one's script. We also examined each of these concepts as part of the Integrating Adult/Intellect Sheath save intimacy.

Intimacy refers to the ability to establish a genuinely open, honest and authentic connection with another person; a connection that is free from any attempts to manipulate or deceive, either psychologically or emotionally. People generally shy away from intimacy because it involves risk; in an intimate relationship, people are vulnerable, and exposed to the possibility of getting hurt. Many prefer safer, more predictable ways of psychologically structuring their time with others, such as withdrawal, rituals, pastimes and activities. Then, too, there are script compulsions that make people play destructive psychological games with each other to reinforce ingrained beliefs about themselves and others (For a detailed discussion of these, the interested reader can refer to my earlier book). In short, poor intimacy doesn't stand much of a chance, although it is held to be the most psychologically rewarding form of time structuring!

"Intimacy" was the word originally used by Eric Berne, but, because of its sexual connotations, some TA writers use the term "closeness" (Hay, 2009) or "connection" (Cook, 2022). Berne conceived of intimacy as the release or recovery of ability or a capacity, as if it was already there within us. In the Vedantic Ego States Model, I consider the capacity for intimacy to be located in the Self. Further, some of the means for recovering intimacy in this earthly life are the methods for strengthening the Bliss Sheath, that is, selfless service and Bhakti Yoga, devotion to God. Both give us a sense of connection to something higher than ourselves, as well as give rise to a feeling of inner peace and contentment. (The third method, intensely focused meditation or *Samadhi*, is more a means of realising oneness with the Supreme Being, and is considered possible only at the highest stage of spiritual evolution). The Integrating Adult can be regarded as a process through which we grow to become better human beings: autonomous, authentic and responsible individuals, with a clear conception of right and wrong, and a capacity for giving and receiving love and affection. We become progressively more and more aware of our inner selves, and, in the end, get in touch with our inmost core—the Self. The logical conclusion of complete autonomy and the integrating process is awareness of the soul and the realisation that it is the same in all living creatures. Such a worldview serves to internalize the virtues of compassion and humility. It is ennobling and spiritually uplifting, and teaches us to be compassionate towards other living beings because *"There but for the grace of God go I"*. It is humbling since you realise that the Self is the same in all living creatures and indeed may be a part of a larger Self. Have any of us ever gazed at a glorious sunset over the sea or the rising sun over a mountain range at daybreak? Don't we feel at such times that we are in the presence of something bigger than ourselves, and also feel a connection with that Agency, whatever name we choose to give it? It is in this sense that I view the end result of integration to be spiritual progress. Significantly, in TA, autonomy has been called the "open door to spirituality" (Kandathil and Kandathil, 1997).

Let us now look at intimacy together with Physis in terms of the Vedantic Ego States Model.

Higher and Higher

Evidently, intimacy refers to the ability to empathise at a level beyond mere words, that of feelings and emotions. I believe that the desire for intimacy is essentially a longing for connectedness, as if one mind seeks to connect with another, so that the two relate to each other as one. It has been conceptualized as two people relating to each other in such a way that a third entity is created in which both are largely merged. Let us hold onto this thought for a while and see where it leads.

Such bonding would be occurring at a level deeper than that of the intellect. We may find pleasure in intellectual discourse and in a free and frank exchange of views, but the yearning for closeness at an emotional level springs from something more fundamental. It is acute enough to be called a 'hunger':

> *"The longing for connection is at the root of our healthy human hungers... Autonomy alone does not fully account for this.... It...misses an important focus on human interdependence, the environment, and the transpersonal. I thus offer the concept of connection as an extension to autonomy and encourage practitioners from all fields to seek autonomy and connection.... Connection is significant because it offers...a focus on our holistic entities, and an acknowledgment of our mutual interpersonal, environmental, and transpersonal influences... Exploring together the connection between us (our intersubjectivity) can shine a light into darkness, bringing a new and sometimes spiritual way of connecting in relationship". (Cook, 2022).*

We could think of connection hunger as a primal urge of the Self, whose worldly manifestation is the human desire to love and be loved. At this level, however, it is spiritual and represents a yearning to merge with something greater.

In the words of Swami Vivekananda,

> *"...love—the intense longing for association, the strong desire on the part of two to become one—and, it may be after all, of all to become merged in one—*

> *is being manifested everywhere...” (Vedanta: Voice of Freedom, 1987).*

The Vedantic perspective is that the Self is the abode of pure Bliss and it interprets the worldly manifestation of Bliss as love.

Returning to Physis, in the Vedantic Ego States Model, the arrow representing the inner drive to progress and do better rises upward from the Self beyond the layers of the personality and the physical body. This naturally gives rise to the question: progress towards what?

Brahman

Vedanta uses the conceptualisation of *Sat Chit Ananda* to also characterise the Supreme Principle that has created the universe called Brahman:

> *“In the beginning, my dear, all this [Universe] was Being (Sat) alone, one only without a second”*
>
> *—Chhandogya Upanishad*
>
> *“Brahman is Consciousness”*
>
> *—Aitareya Upanishad*
>
> *“He realised that Bliss (Ananda) is Brahman,*
>
> *For from Bliss, verily, are these beings born,*
>
> *By Bliss, when born, do they live;*
>
> *Into Bliss [at the time of dissolution] do they enter, do they merge”.*
>
> *—Taittiriya Upanishad*

(The above translations are by Paramahansa Yogananda; www. yogananda.au)

Swami Vivekananda puts it most eloquently:

> *“The Vedantist gives no other attributes to God except these three: that He is Infinite Existence, Infinite Knowledge [Consciousness], and Infinite Bliss and he regards these three as one. Existence without Knowledge cannot be. Knowledge without Love and Love without Knowledge cannot be. What we want*

is the harmony of Existence, Knowledge and Bliss Infinite. For that is our goal".

—Vedanta: Voice of Freedom

Apart from these three attributes, there is nothing that can characterise *Brahman*; the *Upanishads* say simply that God (or the Supreme Principle, if you prefer) is "*Neti, Neti*" (not this, not that). It is Unknowable.

And what of the other entity which *Vedanta* characterises as *Sat Chit Ananda*, the *Atman* or Self/Soul? Why, they are the same:

"This Self is Brahman"

—Mandukya Upanishad

"I am Brahman"

—Brihadaranyaka Upanishad

This (in Sanskrit, *Aham Brahmasmi)* is one of the *Mahavakyas* (Great Sayings) of *Vedanta.*

Swami Vivekananda again:

"When Vedanta says that you and I are God, it does not mean the Personal God. To take an example: Out of a mass of clay a huge elephant of clay is manufactured, and out of the same clay, a little clay mouse is made. Would the clay mouse ever be able to become the same as the clay elephant? But put them both in water and they are both clay. As clay they are both one, but as mouse and elephant there will be an eternal difference between them. The Infinite, the Impersonal, is like the clay in the example. We and the Ruler of the Universe are one..."

—Vedanta: Voice of Freedom

The realisation that the Self is alike in all is beautifully articulated in other Vedantic scriptures:

Nidagha, disciple of the sage Ribhu, was one day standing by the side of the street along with other onlookers, watching the royal procession pass on its way to the palace. An old peasant in tattered clothes, standing next to him, touched his arm and said,

"Excuse me, my good sir, what is happening in the street?"

Nidagha replied, "The King, in a royal procession, is going to the palace".

"The King? But where is he?"

Nidagha replied, a trifle irritably, "There, on the elephant".

"But please tell me, which is the king and which is the elephant?"

Nidagha was angry now. "The man above is the king and the animal below is the elephant!" he shouted.

The peasant said, "Above? Below? What does it mean?"

Nidagha yelled at him, "Bend down and I'll show you!" When the peasant did as he was told, Nidagha jumped up on his back.

"Now do you see? I am above as the king and you are below as the elephant! Is it clear?"

"No, not yet" was the reply "King, elephant, above, below; it is clear. But please tell me what you mean by I and You."

Faced with the enormous difficulty of distinguishing "I" from "You", enlightenment came to Nidagha in a flash. He jumped down and fell at the peasant's feet.

"None other than my beloved master Ribhu would have chosen this way to teach me this lesson, to see the true nature of the Self!"

—Ribhu Gita, age unknown

If the Self is the same in both of us, then surely our natural assumption towards ourselves and others must be **I'm OK, You're OK.**

You are That

From the *Upanishads*:

> *"Bring me a fruit of the banyan tree".*
>
> *"Here it is, Father".*
>
> *"Break it open... what do you see?"*
>
> *"These tiny seeds".*
>
> *"Now break one open... what do you see?"*
>
> *"Nothing, Father".*
>
> *"My son... there is a subtle essence which you do not perceive, but through the essence the truly immense banyan tree exists... It is Truth. It is the Self; and you are that" (Tat Tvam Asi in the original Sanskrit).*
>
> —*Chhandogya Upanishad*

"Tat Tvam Asi" is another *Mahavakya* of *Vedanta*.

Recall that in Chapter II, we had briefly mentioned the *Purushartha* or goals of life. One of them is *Moksha* or spiritual perfection. Now, *Vedanta* says that the highest form of *Moksha* is the liberation of the Self from the cycle of births and deaths (The Sanskrit word *"Moksha"* literally means "release" or "liberation"). Physis, as the inner drive to grow and become better, arising from the Self, can be viewed as an urge to reach perfection—physical, mental, emotional and finally spiritual. And so, the growth arrow of Physis ultimately represents the striving of the Self to attain the ultimate in spiritual perfection, that is, the merger of the Self with God *(Brahman)*. It is relevant to mention that in one of the TA models, this arrow is shown as located within a hollow core common to all three ego states (Tigchelaar, 2019).

Also, as we have seen, intimacy was represented *as the merging of two personalities together into a third entity.* Recalling Swami Vivekananda's statement about *the longing of all to become merged in one,* we arrive at the ultimate destination of Physis given above.

(However, in this book, we will be more concerned with our earthly life in the here and now, and keep in mind that the drive to become better is a journey, not a destination. We shall see later how we can get the most out of our journey.)

When the merging is achieved, the Self does not manifest anymore in the world but stays in *Brahman* in eternal *Sat Chit Ananda*.

On the worldly level, *Moksha* also means enlightenment and spiritual mastery, and we shall see later how to achieve this along with the other goals of life; *Vedanta* enjoins us to pursue all four *Purusharthas* (goals) in a balanced manner.

What's Love Got to Do With It?

The sceptic will say, "This is all very well, but how does *Vedanta* bring love into this equation of *Atman* and *Brahman*? Love, after all, is a worldly emotion, experienced by human beings within their lifetime". To answer this, let us invent an imaginary Socratic dialogue on the subject in the modern age. Just for fun, we will take Socrates' opponent to be an actual historical figure, Protagoras the Sophist, who has lent his name to the word "protagonist":

Socrates: So, my dear Protagoras, you do not admit that there is any such thing as spiritual love.

Protagoras: Indeed I do not, Socrates. It has been conclusively shown that the feeling we call love is due to the production of certain chemicals like oxytocin and serotonin. It is purely a biological phenomenon.

Soc: But how are these chemicals produced?

Prot: By the brain.

Soc: And how does the brain know when to produce them?

Prot: Upon receiving sense-impressions, for example, when the mother sees her baby or the lover grasps the hand of the beloved.

Soc: How does the mother see?

Prot: What a question, Socrates! With her eyes, of course.

Soc: But that, my good sir, is not my meaning. I want to know what it is in the eyes that make the mother see.

Prot: She is awake and conscious, and so she sees her baby.

Soc: And where does this consciousness come from?

Prot: From the brain.

Soc: Does it? Are you aware that according to modern neuroscience, there are presently twenty two theories of how consciousness arises in the brain involving neurons and neural networks in different areas of the brain? This is the same as the scientists saying that they do not know. No, my friend, *consciousness is what gives life to the brain; therefore, it must come from an agency other than the brain.* A dead brain would receive no sense-impressions whatsoever.

Prot: So tell me, Socrates, you who are so fond of asking questions: where does consciousness come from?

Soc: It comes from the soul that breathes life into the body, that which the wise men of India call *Atman.*

Prot: Let us say that you are right. What does Love have to do with all this?

Soc: If the soul gives life to the brain and the brain produces the love chemicals, then in the final analysis it is the soul that creates love. Indeed, the same wise men say that the soul dwells in a state of bliss, which manifests in the human being as love. They also say that it is only a reflection of the World Soul, the Consciousness that has created the universe and that the soul longs to merge into the World Soul, which they call *Brahman.* In fact, *all* souls long to merge in Brahman, which dwells in a state of permanent bliss. This, my friend, is the purest, most spiritual expression of love!

A small game, such as children and philosophers play, will make it easier to visualise this. Imagine that we reverse the *Pancha Kosha* model, so that the Food Sheath is the innermost, enclosed by the Vital Air Sheath. This in turn is enclosed by the Mental Impressions Sheath, which is contained within the Intellect Sheath. This is enclosed by the Bliss Sheath, and beyond the Bliss Sheath is the Self, which is unconfined (Fig. 4.1).

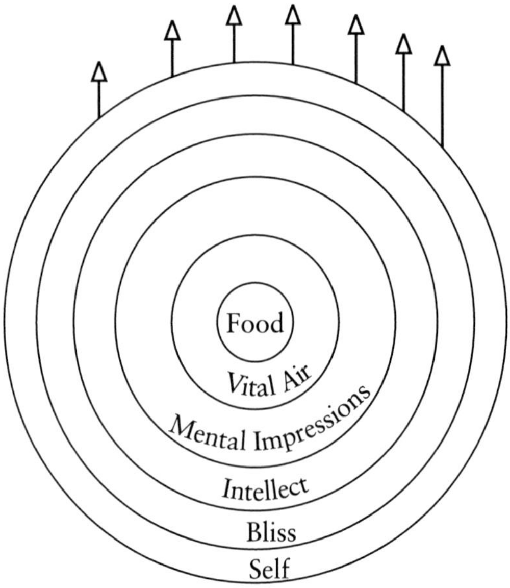

Fig. 4.1: *Pancha Kosha* Reversed

In this case, we are progressing outward from the corporeal to the invisible, from matter to energy and from the gross to the subtle. We can see the body, we can feel the breath, but beyond that our sense-impressions give way to energy fields of mental impressions and the intellect and finally the purely spiritual. The Bliss Sheath, of course, is but a reflection of the unconfined Self, which is represented as being everywhere. The arrows rising up from it are the arrows of Physis. On one level, they show us trying to achieve perfection; on the earthly level, it is an affirmation of self-love also, the recognition that I am a unique being with a unique, God-given talent that it is my sacred duty to discover and that I have something to give to the world...in other words, that I am OK. On the Vedantic level, they show us trying to reach the World Soul with...a Love Supreme!

"I belong to no religion
My religion is love
Every heart is my temple"

—Gautama Buddha, c. 6th century BCE

5
The *Vedantic* Worldview

"Do not look at anybody in terms of friend or foe, brother or cousin; do not fritter away your mental energies in thoughts of friendship or enmity. Seeking the Self everywhere, be amiable and equal-minded towards all, treating all alike"

—Adi Shankara, spiritual guru, c. 8th century CE.

In the Introduction, I had acknowledged that *Vedanta* is an ocean and I am barely skimming its surface in this book. Indeed, many saints, sages and spiritual seekers have written marvellously about it over the centuries and their works explain much more about *Vedanta*, and do far greater justice to its subtleties than I can. I have briefly discussed some of the Vedantic concepts, which we will now look at in greater detail, in addition to discussing a few other important ones. Wherever possible, I will relate it to the TA framework.

Purushartha

Purushartha, the meaning or objective of life, comprises four goals:

- *Dharma*
- *Artha*
- *Kama*
- *Moksha*

Dharma in this context is of two types: *Sadharana dharma,* which roughly means one's duties, obligations and responsibilities as members of a family, community and culture. *Svadharma* means one's own particular responsibility to oneself and has been explained as the lawful conduct of self based on the identification of one's own ability.

Here we can see where the actualisation of potential comes in. We have a sacred duty to ourselves to find out what we are good at and try to excel in it. We also have the freedom to work out our own *(sva)dharma,* which may at times conflict with our *sadharana dharma;* indeed, the *Bhagavad Gita*, the holiest scripture of Hinduism, dwells at length on the clash between the two.

It is evident that *sadharana dharm*a is handed down to us by our parents and other authority figures and forms a part of the Parent ego state including the Cultural Parent. It also forms a part of the Adapted Child ego state, since as children we learned ways of behaving that would satisfy our parents' expectations from us, in addition to learning how to behave in society, etc. However, in the Vedantic Ego States Model, both Parent and Child are located within the Mental Impressions Sheath, which is subservient to the Intellect Sheath. This means that if I apply my intellect with all the wisdom at its command, I can overrule my earlier mental impressions of "doing the right thing" according to my *sadharana dharma* and actually do the right thing according to the *svadharma* I have worked out. This is the formidable power of the intellect, there for us to use but very often sadly neglected.

In fact, one of the best uses of the intellect would be to consciously examine the dictates of our Cultural Parent, and use our own wisdom to decide what can be retained and what can be discarded on grounds of irrelevance or being outdated or harmful.

As an example, when I was writing my earlier book on TA, I wanted to provide an illustration of pastimes, and I wrote that at a dinner party, men may spend time discussing politics, sports and cars, while women may pass time discussing fashion, movies and the fine arts. My mentor and guide in TA, Julie Hay, gently pointed out to me that the illustration was inappropriate.

I was startled to realise that she was quite right, and just how deep-rooted stereotyping can be in the Cultural Parent; the example I had used unthinkingly as a matter of course was indeed sexist and discriminatory. I quickly replaced the example with a safe gender-neutral one.

Of course, the intellect also helps us in figuring out what we are good at, through experimenting, listening to experts, getting other perspectives, reflection and introspection. Another aspect of *svadharma* can be interpreted as striving for excellence in the chosen field.

We can relate this to the Hierarchy of Needs developed by the American psychologist Abraham Maslow (1908–70) shown in Fig. 5.1 as follows:

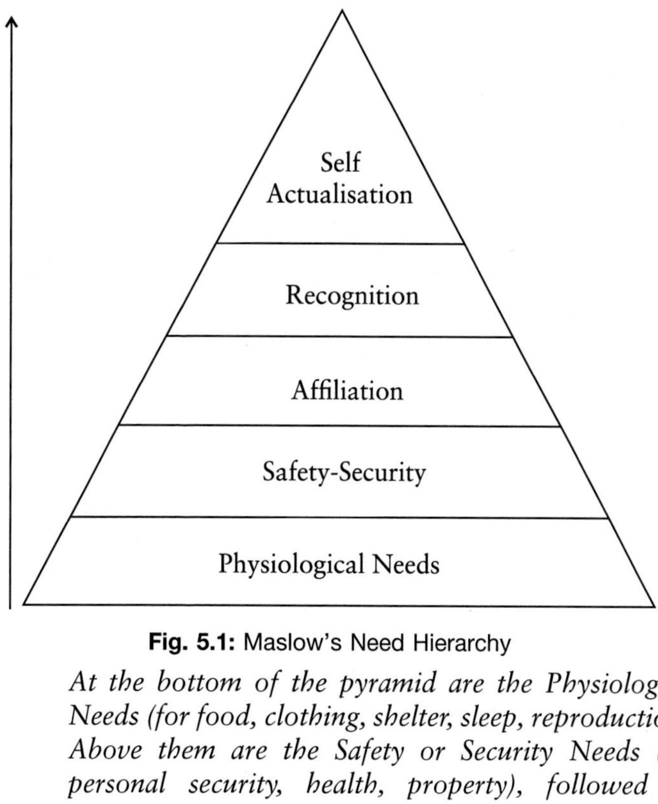

Fig. 5.1: Maslow's Need Hierarchy

At the bottom of the pyramid are the Physiological Needs (for food, clothing, shelter, sleep, reproduction). Above them are the Safety or Security Needs (for personal security, health, property), followed by

Affiliation Needs (for love, family, and friends). Higher than these are the Recognition Needs (for respect, status, self-esteem). At the top of the pyramid is the Self-Actualisation Need (the desire to become the best that one can be).

The original principle was that lower-order needs have to be adequately satisfied before higherorder needs are felt. However, it is now recognised that higher and lower order needs can coexist side by side. This in turn implies that the highest need for self-actualisation is always there, which fits in with the Vedantic view that it is an intrinsic part of the Self. Also, figuring out one's Svadharma and then striving for excellence in it, is part of the need for self-actualisation.

Other contexts in which *dharma* is expressed are as follows:

Satya Dharma, the *dharma* of eternal truth, not just transient information or opinions.

Atma Dharma, the *dharm*a of self-realisation, reveals the divine self that dwells in the hearts of all.

Brahma Dharma, the *dharm*a of *Brahman*, the boundless reality of *sat,* eternal being, *chit,* all-knowing consciousness, and *ananda,* supreme bliss.

Moksha Dharma, grants liberation from all death and sorrow, not just the freedom to pursue outer desires.

Yoga Dharma, including all the paths of yoga as *Karma, Bhakti, Jnana* and *Raja,* as yoga is the traditional way of fulfilling our *Moksha Dharma.*

Veda Dharma, refers to transcendent knowledge imparted by the sages and seers, with *Vedanta* as its prime philosophy.

Vishva Dharma or the Universal *Dharma* is relevant to all living beings and all worlds in the cosmos, from the physical to higher realms beyond name and form.

Manava Dharma, the *dharma* for all human beings, not just for one community, who are all manifestations of the same *Atman.*

Artha means the acquisition of wealth. Spirituality is not found, nor *dharma* obeyed, on an empty stomach. *Vedanta* regards the lawful pursuit of material gain as a noble objective in itself:

Even today, most Hindu shopkeepers, no matter how small their establishments, keep a sign prominently displayed that reads:

"SHUBH LABH"

The literal meaning is "auspicious profit"; profit made lawfully in accordance with principles of ethics and morality. Material well-being is a basic necessity for everyone, and it is right and proper for people to seek artha when they marry and raise a family, so that they can discharge their responsibilities to spouses and children.

On a macroscopic level, the acquisition of wealth is indispensable for a kingdom. In fact, an ancient treatise on statecraft, the *Arthashastra*, discusses in elaborate detail the ways and means by which the king can acquire wealth. From the king's point of view, this preserves the social order and prevents lawlessness.

Kama means enjoying the pleasures of the senses. The term has acquired sexual connotations due to the notoriety of the *Kamasutra,* usually misunderstood as a manual on sex, but its wider meaning covers sense-enjoyment, emotional fulfilment and delighting in aesthetics. It also refers to love and connection, and enjoyment of love with or without sex. We have seen how the connection hunger in TA terms refers to *"an acknowledgment of our mutual interpersonal, environmental, and transpersonal influences"* (Cook, 2022). We have also seen how love is *"the intense desire of the two to become one and, it may be, of all to become merged in one..."* (Swami Vivekananda, 1987). It is not difficult to put the two together and conclude that *Kama,* connection hunger, and love, are one and the same.

"But wait!" the sceptic will cry, "What about sex, the instinct that human beings share with animals? Surely there is nothing spiritual about it when the birds, bees and animals also do it? Further, in human beings, in many cases, it is born of lust, completely antithetical to spirituality!"

To answer this: Sex in nonhuman species is for the purpose of procreation and there is definitely something spiritual about producing a new life, whether driven by instinct or by conscious volition. Secondly, sex in the human world is an expression of love, the desire for "connectedness" manifesting at a physically intimate level. And the desire for connectedness, in its purest form, is "transpersonal" or spiritual, a love supreme.

Lust, according to *Vedanta,* is born of ignorance *(avidya)* of our true nature as spiritual beings. It has no place in *Kama.* Further, the pleasure derived from sex sparked by lust is purely ephemeral, as wonderfully described by one writer:

"Under such circumstances, sex becomes like a sneeze, only involving the lower parts of the body rather than the upper".

Leaving *Moksha* aside for the moment, what it boils down to is that in this life, it is necessary and desirable to acquire *Artha* and enjoy *Kama* within the framework of *Sadharana Dharma.* In other words, it is perfectly OK to gain wealth honestly and lawfully and delight in the pleasures of the senses as long as it is according to acceptable social norms.

Moksha has already been discussed earlier; in its purest form, it refers to the urge of the Self to merge into the World Self.

This is illustrated in the following fable:

Search Within

A long time ago, human beings were endowed with divine powers and were as Godlike as the Gods themselves. But, rejoicing in their divinity, they grew very powerful, and ultimately dared to challenge the Gods themselves for ruling over Heaven and Earth. In order to punish them for their arrogance, the King of the Gods decided to take away their divinity and hide it in a secret place where they would never be able to find it.

"Hide it in the deepest part of the ocean" one God suggested.

"They would dive down and find it", said the King of the Gods.

"Well then, bury it deep in the Earth", suggested another.

He shook his head, "They would dig a tunnel and find it".

Thinking over the matter, he decided that the best thing to do was to hide their divinity inside each human being, deep down at the very core where they would never think of looking for it.

"But if they do search within themselves and discover it: what then?" another God asked.

He smiled "Why then—they will be fit to be Gods themselves".

Returning to the earthly context, *Moksha* means spiritual enlightenment or the search for spiritual perfection. One might, for example, say that those who follow the path of *Bhakti* Yoga and virtually lose themselves in their devotion to God are attaining a form of *Moksha*. Those who regularly keep up their spiritual practice through yoga and meditation can also be considered enlightened in the sense that they are less likely to be swayed by instincts and passions, and more likely to remain calm and tranquil and heed the dictates of reason.

I believe that knowledge of the *Purushartha* or meaning of life according to *Vedanta* will be of utmost benefit to those who consider their lives to be empty, purposeless and devoid of meaning; the candidates for the psychiatrist's couch, to use a cliché. It also provides a new perspective on life that should be conducive to everyone's well-being. Additionally, the varied meanings of *dharma*, as given earlier, serve as guideposts to remind us how we should conduct ourselves in this life.

Rin (Indebtedness)

Everyone of us is under five types of *Rin* (indebtedness) and *Vedanta* says that we should repay these debts as far as possible in our time on the planet. Let us see how:

Deva Rin, debts to the gods and goddesses, can be interpreted to mean the debt to that which has given us the gifts of sun, air, water, light and so on and that which has given us the gift of being able to live in this world and endowed us with consciousness and free will. In other words, it is our debt to the Supreme Principle. It is repaid by diligently keeping up one's spiritual practice through yoga, meditation and observance of *Yama* (vows) and *Niyama* (rules) for spiritual development (Ref. Table 1.1).

Rishi Rin, debts to the seers and sages. This is repaid by absorbing and utilising the wisdom they taught us, and faithful observance of the rites and rituals prescribed by them.

Pitri Rin, debts to parents and ancestors. We repay this by respectfully paying homage to them and honouring and obeying them.

Nri Rin, debts to humanity at large. To repay this, we have to follow the Vedantic principle of "*Vasudaiva Kutumbakam*", which means that "*the whole world* [of human beings] *is my family*". This in turn implies that there is no difference between "I" and "You" (as described in the story in the *Ribhu Gita* in Chapter IV), and both equally deserve the same respect and the same treatment.

A schematic diagram of *Rin* and its constituents is given as follows (Fig. 5.2).

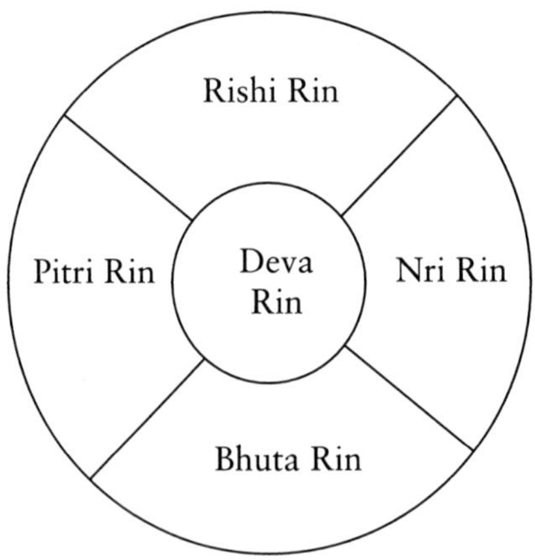

Fig. 5.2: Rin (Indebtedness)

Life Positions

In TA, the concept of life positions assumes that every individual has a preferred life position or psychological assumption about oneself and others, into which they relapse when under stress. The healthiest and most desirable position is considered to be **I'm OK, You're OK**: You are as much worthy of respect and attention as I am.

It is relevant to mention here that Eric Berne believed as a principle that every child is born in the "I'm OK, You're OK" position, although a later TA writer disagreed with him and contended that a child's natural position is I'm Not OK, You're OK. I support Berne's view (which also squares with the Vedantic perspective as we have seen) and can offer the following personal anecdote as evidence:

> *My wife taught in a Montessori school for many years, working with children in the age group eighteen to thirty months. A game the children would play was to throw a ball into a basket placed on the floor near them, turn by turn. Once, during this game, a child with special needs was unable to do it. He tried again and again, growing red with frustration, but no luck. Suddenly one of the children ran up to the basket, picked it up, and brought it and set it down near him so that he could do it. Then she ran back and took her place beside the teacher.*
>
> *The boy threw the ball into the basket and gave a huge smile as the children applauded him.*
>
> *The children with special needs in her class sometimes had trouble taking the Montessori material to work on, although it was kept on low shelves within easy reach. The other children would help them, pushing it nearer where they could get it or picking it up and giving it to them.*

And these are children in the age group 18–30 months we're talking about!

Nri Rin also addresses the concern that some later TA practitioners have raised, that the objective of TA should be homonomy instead of autonomy, on the grounds that autonomy is too individualistic a concept, and homonomy, or viewing oneself as part of a connected whole, is what we should strive for (Tudor, 2011). The same concept has been renamed connectedness (Cook, 2022), which has already been discussed in Chapter IV as a primal urge of the Self, and therefore innate to human beings and waiting to be rediscovered. Did not Plato say that all knowledge is recollection? It fits the *Vedantic* worldview that we have to rediscover our true nature by removing the veil of ignorance.

Bhuta Rin, debts to plants, animals and the environment, is repaid by being considerate towards them and being careful not to disturb the natural order of things. Human interventions need to be limited to repairing the damage caused by us and encouraging the preservation of the ecosystem. A trite example is the water bottle episode given in Chapter II. Soil conservation and enrichment, tree plantation, wildlife conservation, and reduction of greenhouse gas emissions are other more meaningful examples.

Recently a concern has been raised that TA was ignoring the healing power of ecology and the environment. This is sought to be addressed by introducing the concept of "Ecological TA", which is:

> *"an approach for understanding human and more-than-human experience that is forged in connection with the ecological context in which it occurs. Furthermore... this interconnected process incorporates the embodied agency of both human and the more-than-human participants in the encounter. It is, to be more succinct, the practice of transactional analysis in alliance with Earth" (Barrow and Marshall, 2020).*

It is interesting and instructive to see TA getting closer and closer to *Vedanta* through the development of these ideas.

However, now it becomes necessary to discuss some other concepts of *Vedanta* for which there is no TA equivalent or even approximation. This will help us to get an idea of this most subtle of metaphysics.

Maya

The meaning of *Maya* is generally understood to be "Illusion", as in "this world is *Maya*", but actually the concept is more complex. We will turn to one of the greatest sages of the Vedantic tradition, Swami Vivekananda, to describe it in its true sense:

> *"... the Maya of Vedanta, in its last developed form... is a simple statement of fact... what we are and what we see around us... there is the tremendous fact of death... and yet ...we do not know why, we cling to life... this is Maya.... The knowledge of happiness brings the knowledge of unhappiness... The least amount of material prosperity that we enjoy is causing the same amount of misery elsewhere ... And this is Maya... Maya is a statement of the fact of the universe... that the very basis of our being is contradiction, and that everywhere we have to move through this tremendous contradiction, that wherever there is good, there also must be evil... and everyone who smiles will have to weep, and vice versa".*
>
> (*Vedanta: Voice of Freedom*)

This is *Maya*. Happiness and sorrow, pleasure and pain, good and evil, are inextricably intertwined in this world. That's how it is. How should we know pleasure if we did not know pain? How should we know good if we did not know evil? Everything is mixed up together in this world and the grand composition of all these elements is *Maya*.

We find the same vision in the work of the French philosopher Voltaire (1694–1778). Will Durant writes:

> *In "The World As it Goes", Voltaire tells how an angel sent Babouc to report on whether the city of Persepolis should be destroyed; Babouc goes, and is horrified with the vices he discovers; but after a time he began to grow fond of a city the inhabitants of which were polite, affable and beneficent, though they were fickle, slanderous and vain. He was much afraid that the city of Persepolis would be condemned. He was even afraid to give in his account. This he did,*

> *however, in the following manner: He caused a little statue, composed of different metals, of earth and of stones (the most precious and the most vile) to be cast by one of the best founders of the city, and carried it to the angel. "Wilt thou break", said he, "this pretty statue because it is not composed wholly of gold and diamonds?" The angel resolved to think no more of destroying Persepolis but to leave "the world as it goes".*
>
> *(Will Durant, The Story of Philosophy)*

Karma

Karma also has many shades of meaning in different contexts. In its simplest form, it means "work". It also means "work best suited to one's ability" and "actions" and "consequences of actions". We can think of the latter in terms of merits and demerits, and good deeds earn merits and bad deeds earn demerits. But for whom?

According to *Vedanta*, at the time of death, only the physical body dies and the energy fields remain, associated with the Self that is deathless and which takes birth in another body. The sum total of the merits and the sum total of the demerits in a person's life also remain with the Self, and get carried forward to the new life. This is called *karma,* in the sense of consequences of our actions in the world.

The bad *karma* has to be worked off through suffering in this or succeeding lifetimes until the merits balance the demerits, whereupon the Self does not take birth again in this "vale of tears" but instead merges with the World Self and reposes in eternal bliss.

Some critics argue that this is a fatalistic worldview and a negation of free will. If everything I have to suffer or enjoy is already predetermined by my previous lifetimes, what is the use of my striving for anything in this life? I should accept whatever comes my way with resignation, thinking "Oh! It's my *karma* and there is no getting away from it".

Such an argument misses the point entirely because *karma* refers to both action and the consequences of that action. God has given us the gift of free will to choose our actions, but the choice comes at a price:

> *"Karma is the eternal assertion of human freedom;... Our thoughts, our words, and deeds are threads of the net which we throw around ourselves"*
>
> *—Swami Vivekananda*

The most important thing about *karma* is the **simultaneity** of cause and effect. Good actions generate good *karma* and bad actions generate bad *karma*. Every choice of action or speech or behaviour has a consequence. This is a universal truth:

> *"As ye sow, so shall ye reap"*
>
> *—Holy Bible*

This principle is well illustrated in the following story:

A Pound of Butter

Once there was a farmer who sold a pound of butter to a baker. One day the baker decided to weigh the butter to see if he was getting a pound and he found he was not. This angered him and he took the farmer to the court.

The judge asked the farmer if he was using any measure. The farmer replied, "Your Honour, I am primitive. I don't have a proper measure but I do have a scale".

"Then how do you weigh the butter?" the judge asked.

The farmer replied, "Your Honour, long before the baker started buying butter from me, I have been buying a loaf of bread weighing one pound from him. Everyday when the baker brings the bread, I put it on the scale and give him the same weight in butter. If anyone is to be blamed, it is the baker".

If I want to create happiness in my life, I must learn to sow the seeds of happiness. Therefore, I have a choice; in other words, I have free will.

Choices

High in the Himalayas lived a wise old man. Periodically, he ventured down into the local village to entertain the villagers with his special knowledge and talents. One of his skills was to "psychically" tell the villagers the contents in their pockets, boxes or minds.

A few young boys from the village decided to play a joke on the wise old man and discredit his special abilities. One boy came up with the idea to capture a bird and hide it in his hands. He knew, of course, the wise old man would know that the object in his hands was a bird.

The plan was that the boy would ask the old man if the bird was dead or alive. If he said the bird was alive, the boy would crush the bird in his hands, so that when he opened his hands the bird would be dead. If the wise man said the bird was dead, the boy would open his hands and show him that it was alive. So, no matter what the old man said, the boy would prove him a fraud.

The following week, the wise old man came down from the mountains again. The boy quickly caught a bird and cupping it out of sight in his hands, walked up to him and asked, "Old man, old man, what is it that I have in my hands?"

The old man said, "You have a bird", and he was right.

The boy then asked, "Old man, old man, tell me, is the bird alive or is it dead?"

The wise old man looked at the boy and said, "The bird is as you choose it".

As the boy looked at him dumbfounded, the old man added quietly, "And so it is with your life".

If I make a good choice, my soul accumulates good *karma*, whose benefit "I" (my soul) will reap in this or a later lifetime. If I make a bad choice, I accumulate bad *karma,* whose consequences I will suffer in this or a later lifetime. And our planet is actually a school, where the soul goes to learn its lessons and to evolve spiritually.

But the learning comes afterwards and life happens before that; to paraphrase Oscar Wilde,

"Life is a hard school; it gives you the experience first and the lesson afterwards"

The "grading" of the lessons is, of course, the *karma* that accumulates both good and bad.

Another story may help in appreciating this subtle Vedantic concept:

The Fence

There was a boy who had a foul temper and used to get angry very often. One day his father took him to the backyard and told him,

"Do you see this fence? Every time you get angry I want you to hammer a nail into it".

The first day the boy had hammered fifty two nails into the fence. The second day it was thirtyfive, the third day twenty three, and so on. Eventually there came a day when the boy was able to tell his father,

"Today I didn't hammer any nails into the fence."

"Very good, son" his father said, "And now, for every day that you don't lose your temper, I want you to pull out one of the nails".

This was a tough job, but eventually the boy was able to proudly tell his father,

"I've pulled all the nails out. I don't lose my temper anymore".

His father took him to the backyard again:

"Son, you don't lose your temper anymore, that's fine. But do you see the scars on the fence?"

"So it is with hurtful deeds and words. You can apologize and take them back, but the scars will remain, even as the scars from the nails remain on the fence."

If we consider the fence to be the Self and the nails our harmful deeds, the scars are the negative karma we accumulate.

They don't go away and we have to pay the price for them, in this lifetime or another.

Nishkama Karma: Renunciation in Action

When we speak of karma in the sense of "work" or "duty", the central message of *Vedanta* is that we should work without expecting any reward for our labour, that is, work without any motive. This is called the doctrine of *nishkama karma,* which literally means "working without desire".

A friend told me the following:

> *I had an attack of Covid that affected my central nervous system to the extent that I had long-term problems with balance and started using a walking stick for stability. Regular physiotherapy helped somewhat but I was still shaky. I started going for a walk in the evenings with my wife, moving slowly because of the stick, with the belief that the more I walked, the better my muscles would obey my brain.*
>
> *One day while walking in the neighbourhood, a security guard, a complete stranger, came running up to me. He said, "Sir, you need to have the juice of the Giloy plant (heart-shaped moonflower) leaves and you will be perfectly cured".*
>
> *I stopped and looked at him: "Where do I get it?"*
>
> *The guard said, "It grows wild. I'll get some for you if you want".*
>
> *The next evening when I was walking with my wife, the guard gave me a packet of the leaves, saying, "It grows near my house; I brought some for you" and proceeded to give my wife instructions for preparing and administering the juice.*

My friend said, "I didn't know the guy and had never seen him before. On his own, he offered to help. When I started drinking the juice, he told me that he would give me some more *Ayurvedic* (traditional medicine) remedies to cure my condition".

The guard had no motive and no expectation behind the help that he offered, and no thought of reward. This is *nishkama karma.*

We should work (do our duty) impersonally, without the sense that "I am performing this work". Looking at it another way, the doctrine of *Karma* Yoga enjoins us to work with full concentration, losing the sense of identity altogether:

> *"If a painter, losing the consciousness of his ego, becomes completely immersed in his painting, he will be able to produce masterpieces. A good cook concentrates his whole self on the food he handles. Then he loses consciousness of everything else for the time being... The Gita teaches that all work should be done thus. He who is one with the Lord through yoga performs all his work by becoming immersed in concentration, and does not seek any personal benefit.... He works best who works without any motive—neither for money, nor for fame, nor for anything else".*
>
> *—Swami Vivekananda*

A master worker works for the sake of his craft. We are told that when Michelangelo painted the ceiling of the Sistine Chapel, he did so in a fury of ecstasy and concentration, lying on his back on precarious scaffolding, not caring for splashing paint on his face and clothes. The accomplished dancer loses herself in her art, not caring for the response from the audience or the money she is going to earn for displaying her talent.

According to *Vedanta*, all work should be performed in this spirit, whether the worker is skilled or not.

There is more, however: the work (*karma*) should be performed as a sacrifice to the Lord, as an act of worship:

> *"This world is the cause of the bondage of karma, except for actions performed for the purpose of sacrifice. Therefore... perform actions for the sake of sacrifice and conduct yourself as free from attachment".*
>
> *—Bhagavad Gita, trans. Swami Rama*

We note in passing that the credo of "work is worship" was also highlighted by the sociologist Max Weber in *The Protestant Ethic and the Spirit of Capitalism,* although he interpreted it as the driving force behind the rise of capitalism and free enterprise in the 18th and 19th centuries.

To return to choices; all of us are essentially choicemakers; some are conscious and some are unconscious. From TA we remember that many of our unconscious choices result from programming in our subconscious that we are not aware of. As such, we cannot evaluate these choices in terms of good or bad, and they have the potential to lead us astray in terms of creating bad *karma*. The TA therapist uncovers this programming in her clients through therapy sessions and shows them how they can change it. However, there are many people who do not go to therapists but end up creating bad *karma* for themselves through the unconscious choices they make. Can the principles of *Vedanta,* coupled with our knowledge of TA, do anything for them? They can, and in the following chapter, we will see how.

6
Taking Charge

"The insights and understandings of the perennial psychology of the Bhagavad Gita can do much to enrich modern psychology and psychotherapy"

—Swami Rama, Perennial Psychology of the Bhagavad Gita

We have come a long way in our journey, delving into the depths of the human soul beyond the trappings of the personality as well as exploring the grandeur of the Creator of the Universe or the Supreme Principle, if you will. We have learned the Vedantic perspective that the merger of the former with the latter, achieved over several lifetimes, is the ultimate objective of the soul in its quest for spiritual perfection. This objective can be achieved by following the various prescribed paths of Yoga.

We have a choice, whether to try to attain the ultimate in spiritual liberation (*Moksha*) through the various prescribed paths,

Or

to revere and pay homage to the Spirit within all of us, and try to attain happiness and grow to our full potential in this lifetime.

The divergence begins from the Intellect Sheath:

> *"Two roads diverged in a wood, and I—I took the road less travelled..."*
>
> *—Robert Frost, The Road Not Taken*

This is, however, the way of the *yogi*. Generally, the majority of us just want to live a happy and fulfilling life in this existence, earning good *karma* and growing to our full potential in our time on Planet Earth. This choice is also perfectly OK!

Let us examine how *Vedanta* can help us achieve our objective, keeping in mind the insights gained from TA. For this, it is worthwhile to refresh the Vedantic Ego States Model, to see how we can get the utmost benefit from it and also to summarise what we have discussed about *Vedanta* so far:

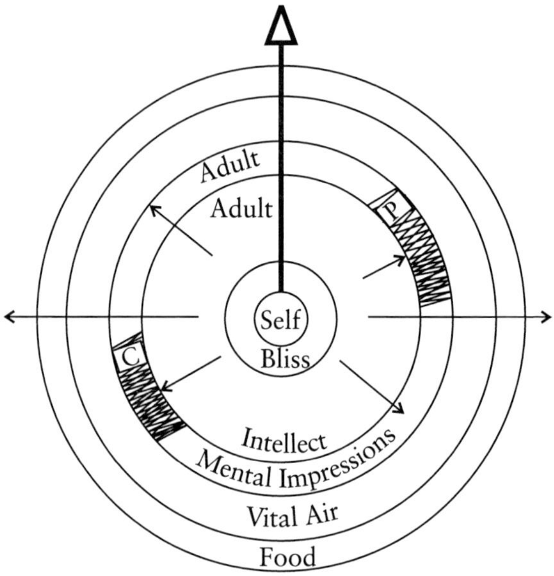

Fig. 6.1: Vedantic Ego States Model

P = Parent
C = Child

Recall that the Sheath of Mental Impressions is controlled by the Intellect Sheath, which operates on the sheaths enveloping it and also on external reality to pick up external stimuli. It dictates our response to situations, events, thoughts and feelings. It is also home to the higher considerations of ethics, morality and responsibility, as well as willpower.

Developing the intellect leads to increased control over our thoughts, feelings and behaviour. It also opens the door for the realisation of the Bliss Sheath and ultimately the Self.

The Self *(Atman)* is the same in all living and nonliving things, and is the same as the Supreme Principle (*Brahman*). Self-realisation means the (spiritual) merger of *Atman* into *Brahman*.

The paths prescribed for Self-realisation are:

- *Karma* Yoga—work as worship without thought of reward
- *Jnana* Yoga—strengthening the intellect
- *Bhakti* Yoga—Devotion to the Supreme Principle, love of humanity, selfless service
- *Raja* Yoga—concentrated meditation, tranquillity.

The principles of *Rin* or indebtedness:

- To the Supreme Principle for the gifts of air, water, sunlight, etc.
- To the sages for the wisdom they imparted
- To our ancestors and parents who made us what we are
- To humanity at large for the qualities that make us human and our common Self-hood
- To nonhuman and nonliving things (ecology and environment)

During our lifetime, we should discharge these debts to the extent possible.

The *Purushartha* or objectives of life:

Legitimate acquisition of wealth (*artha*) and enjoyment of the pleasures of the senses (*kama*) within the framework of one's duties, responsibilities and obligations (*dharma*).

To discover one's unique abilities and achieve excellence in the same (*svadharm*a).

To attain a state of spiritual excellence (*moksha*).

Practise being a witness to our actions, thoughts and feelings.

Accept that the world is full of contradictions (*Maya*) and that we have to navigate through life as best we can.

The Butterfly

A man found a cocoon of a butterfly. One day a small opening appeared in the cocoon through which the butterfly was trying to come out. He sat and watched the butterfly for several hours as it struggled to force its body through the hole. Then it seemed to stop making any progress, and appeared to have gone as far as it could, and then given up.

The man decided to help the butterfly, and with scissors snipped off the rest of the cocoon. The butterfly could then emerge easily, but it had a swollen body and shrivelled wings. He watched, expecting the wings to grow and the body to shrink. But this did not happen, and the butterfly spent the rest of its life crawling around with a swollen body and deformed wings. It was never able to fly.

The man in his kindness and haste did not understand that the restricting cocoon and the struggle required for the butterfly to emerge from the small opening helps to force the fluid from its body into the wings. This results in making the wings stronger and also in draining its swelled body. This process makes the butterfly ready to fly after coming out of its cocoon.

Sometimes, struggles are exactly what we need in life.

We are endowed with freedom of choice as regards our thoughts, feelings and behaviour.

However, this freedom comes at a price. Good actions earn merit (good *karma*) that will be enjoyed through good fortune in this or succeeding lifetimes, and bad actions earn demerits (bad *karma*) that must be worked off through suffering in this or successive lifetimes.

But how to make out what is good and what is bad? Is there any such thing as an absolute good or an absolute bad? The sage explains:

> *"The result of every work is mixed with good and evil. There is no good work that has not a touch of evil in it... We should engage in such work as brings*

> *the largest amount of good and the smallest measure of evil... We are reading the Gita by candlelight, but numerous insects are being burned to death... some evil always clings to work. Those who work without any consciousness of their lower ego are not affected by evil... To work without motive, to work unattached, brings the highest bliss and freedom..."*
>
> *—Swami Vivekananda, Vedanta: Voice of Freedom*

Again:

> *"...pay as much attention to the means of work as the end.... With the means all right, the end must come... it is the cause that produces the effect... And unless the causes are exact, proper and powerful, the effect will not be produced".*

This is, of course, diametrically opposite to the Machiavellian doctrine that the end justifies the means. But this is not surprising. *Vedanta* places the greatest value on morality and ethics, which are largely neglected in the Italian diplomat's writings.

The Swamiji, then, has given us guidelines for actions that are good (and, by implication, actions that are bad). Those actions are the best that are determined (by our intellect) to have the maximum good consequences and the least bad consequences. Work should be performed without any motive (of reward) and in a spirit of detachment (as a witness and as an act of worship); this is the doctrine of *nishkama karma.*

A third guideline comes from the meaning of *dharma* as "universal order of things". Our actions must be in conformity with the universal laws of the cosmos. This is a little more subtle and needs a little explanation. We will borrow a leaf from the book of the great German philosopher Immanuel Kant (1724–1804) and his theory of the Categorical Imperative:

> *"Act only according to that maxim whereby you can at the same time will that it should become a universal law".*

—Immanuel Kant, Groundwork of the Metaphysics of Morals

What does this mean? We can lie, we can cheat, we can steal, but we would not wish to live in a world where lying, cheating and stealing are universal laws. And therefore, our conscience *categorically* enjoins us that our actions should be such that they would be capable of being universal laws. This is the basis of morality and ethics.

According to our Vedantic Ego States Model, the Intellect Sheath is home to these higher-order attributes of the personality. If we wish to further develop these qualities in us, we have to strengthen the Intellect Sheath. Also, from the point of view of TA, this would result in strengthening the Integrating Adult, taking us further down the road to autonomy.

Dealing with Thoughts

The path to developing the right ways of thinking is to strengthen the Intellect Sheath.

A woodcutter was cutting a tree. He had been working hard for the last three days. The tree was thick and he felt tired. A traveller was passing by the place where he was busy sawing the tree. He could see the woodcutter was working hard but without much success. He suggested to the woodcutter that he stop cutting the wood for some time and instead sharpen his saw.

The woodcutter got annoyed and said, "Look here, I don't have time to sharpen my saw. I am too busy cutting this tree. Please don't waste my time".

The traveller smiled and went on his way.

In Chapter II, we have discussed the power of the intellect, making specific note of the everyday techniques we can use to develop it, including:

- Isolation
- Introspection
- Self-study and reflection

Reflection *(manan)* has the power of converting knowledge to wisdom, as previously stated. Without reflection, we go blindly on our way, creating unintended consequences that may not be beneficial for us. Therefore, let us spend some time on this all-important technique:

The methods for reflection are as follows:

Questioning: Not taking anything for granted unless it has been properly considered. The Socratic method of asking questions to reveal the truth is a good example. Niels Bohr, one of the founders of modern physics, used to begin his lectures by saying to his students, "Every statement of mine should be regarded by you as a question, not as an assertion".

"I keep six honest serving men,
They taught me all I know,
Their names are Who and What and Why
And Where and When and How"

—Rudyard Kipling

Logical Thinking: Drawing inferences and making deductions from available data, as in mathematical exercises. For example,

(A) Man is a rational animal. (B) Socrates is a man. (C) Therefore, Socrates is a rational animal.

In logic, this is known as a syllogism, with a major premise (A), a minor premise (B) and a conclusion (C).

Lateral Thinking: Creatively thinking "out of the box", allowing the intellect to roam freely and make its own associations unfettered by logic. Brainstorming is an example of this. Another marvellous example from Edward de Bono, who coined the term:

Two Pebbles

A poor farmer was heavily indebted to a moneylender, but could not pay him all at once as the moneylender demanded. He threatened to throw the farmer in jail. Taking the farmer's beautiful young daughter outside, he told her privately:

"Look here, my dear, I'll make you a proposal. I will put a white pebble and a black pebble in this bag, and you must draw one of them without looking.

If you draw a black pebble, I'll waive your father's debt but you'll have to marry me.

If you draw a white pebble, I'll still waive your father's debt, and you won't have to marry me.

If you refuse to draw a pebble, your father goes to jail".

He picked up two pebbles from the garden path and, putting them into a small bag, held it out to the girl, asking her to draw one. However, the sharp-eyed girl noticed that he had picked up two black pebbles.

She obediently drew a pebble from the bag but dropped it on the ground without showing it to the moneylender.

"Oh, I'm sorry, how clumsy of me! I dropped it", she said, "But if you look in the bag, you will see which colour pebble I drew".

Analysis: Examining the data by breaking it down into its constituent parts, for example,

How do you eat an elephant? By cutting it into bite-sized pieces.

Synthesis: Organising the data to bring about an understanding of the whole. By way of an example, we turn once again to the work of Immanuel Kant in *The Critique of Pure Reason,* which can be briefly described thus:

The mind is an active organising agent, and not merely a clean slate on which the senses write their will; it selects and organises sensory data into perceptions, and repeated perceptions into experience. Repeated experiences are organised into information, and aggregated information into knowledge.

Turning Away: Sometimes, concentrating on a problem does not lead to a solution. Engaging in some other activity, for example, going for a walk, shifts the focus while the mind subconsciously keeps engaging with it. A solution can occur in this way. Indeed, there are examples of solutions occurring in dreams also. Such is the power of the intellect!

The German chemist Joseph Kekule (1829–96) was working on the molecular structure of the chemical compound Benzene and had reached a dead end because none of the known molecular structures fitted it. In frustration, he stopped working on it and took up something else. A few days later, at night

he had a dream in which he saw a snake swallowing its tail. The next morning he took up the problem again and thereby discovered not only the structure of benzene but also a hitherto unknown class of closed-chain compounds.

Intuition: The answer occurs in a flash, as in "He had an epiphany". It is also known as the sixth sense:

> *Dmitri Mendeleev (1834–1907), a Russian chemist, was convinced that elements could be arranged according to their atomic weight. He wrote down the names of the elements on cards and used to shuffle them and put them in patterns, a game his friends used to call Patience. He laid them out in tabular form, beginning with the lightest first, and then the second lightest, and so on, in the first row. In the second row, he put elements that were progressively heavier and had similar properties to the ones above them. It worked until the third row; he came to an element next heavier to the one before it in the row, but quite dissimilar to the one above it. Pondering the problem, the answer struck him in a flash; there was a yet undiscovered element that would occupy the position, and when it was found, its weight would be between the two, and its properties would be similar to the one above it!*
>
> *The element was duly discovered later on, and Mendeleev proved right. Till today, he is known as the father of the Periodic Table of Elements.*

We will return to intuition later on, as some Vedantic doctrines speak of it as a property of the Self.

Pitfalls Involved in Reflection

Overthinking: Sometimes, it can be counterproductive to go too deep into a problem and the result can be getting tied up in knots:

> *"The mind of man, if it worketh upon matter... worketh according to the stuff, and is limited thereby; but if it works upon itself, as the spider worketh his web, then it is endless, and brings forth indeed cobwebs*

of learning, admirable for the fineness of thread and work, but of no substance or profit".

—Francis Bacon, The Advancement of Learning

Erroneous Analysis: Coming to a hasty conclusion on the basis of a wrong interpretation, without sufficiently reflecting, is equally problematic:

Market for Shoes

A shoe company wanted to expand its business. The top management decided to send a team of marketing professionals to assess market feasibility in a remote, small and poor country. The team quickly reported back that there was no market for shoes in this country because no one wore shoes. Another shoe company also sent its marketing team to the same place. After a month-long study, the team concluded that the place had great market potential because no one wore shoes.

Procrastinating: Sometimes, we tend to put off making a decision on the plea that we are considering all aspects. It may be useful to set a mental deadline for reflection in such cases.

Lack of Objectivity: Thinking about oneself excessively can render reflection infructuous. We need to put thoughts of self aside and practise detachment when engaged in reflection upon an issue. (As a matter of fact, practising detachment is one of the cornerstones of *Vedanta*).

Limitations of Logic: We need to recognise that logic too has limitations, whether inductive or deductive, and fruitless reasoning can lead us to a dead end. As an example, consider the above syllogism on Socrates being a rational animal. The difficulty is that the conclusion (C) is contained in the major premise (A); for if Socrates is not a rational animal (and no one doubts that he is a man), then Man is not a rational animal.

However, the syllogism is not so much a mechanism for arriving at the truth as it is for the exposition and clarification of knowledge.

How does Reflection Convert Knowledge to Wisdom?

According to the Vedantic perspective, repetition of thought by the Sheath of Mental Impressions creates a desire leading to taking suitable action to fulfill that desire. Repeated cycles of this create a habit.

The Intellect Sheath also repeats thoughts but in a way quite different from the Mental Impressions Sheath. It engages in conscious and deliberate repetition of patterns of thought, followed by reflection, which leaves time and space for making new neural connections, resulting in new associations and new perspectives. The process is facilitated by the methods for reflection outlined above, and the result is wisdom, the quality of having experience, knowledge and good judgement. It is however important to have a period of rest after concentrated thought or sustained reflection. The story of Kekule given earlier is an example of this.

Some Thoughts on Artificial Intelligence

Recently, there has been a lot of interest in Artificial Intelligence (AI) and its capabilities. AI runs on algorithms, which are essentially sets of computer programs that operate on a field of data, which can be all the data in the World Wide Web or the Internet. In this way, it can assemble, put together, take apart, synthesise, process, summarise, analyse, create, and do many other things that we cannot do, with the data available to it. However, AI does not have the ability to reflect, and therefore its role is limited to processing knowledge in accordance with the instructions fed into its program(s). So AI lacks the capacity for wisdom. In the final analysis, it is only technology, albeit amazing technology. And underlying any technological approach is a fundamental ethical and philosophical question about how do we define truth and morality, to whom do we give the power to say what is good and what is bad, what is true and what is false. Technology is not and can never be a solution for that. The solution, if any, can only be found in the higher reaches of the intellect.

Vedanta and TA: Practical Implications

The correspondence between TA and Vedantic concepts is shown as follows:

Table 6.1: Correspondence between TA and Vedantic concepts

S. No.	TA Concept	Vedantic Concept	Remarks
1.	Ego States	Mental Impressions Sheath and Intellect Sheath	Ego states are mental impressions except that part of the Adult that contains the Intellect, which acts as an operator upon the mental impressions
2.	Adult Ego State	Intellect Sheath and part of Mental Impressions Sheath	Intellect operates on external reality, remaining part of Adult, and Parent and Child. Also home to conscience, morality and ethics
3.	Autonomy	Achieved by strengthening of Intellect Sheath	Through various methods of absorption of wisdom, practice of Shreyas and Rin, working out one's personal Dharma
4.	Awareness	Intellect Sheath	Regulates contact between external reality and internal world
5.	Spontaneity	Intellect Sheath	Through functions of judgement and decision
6.	Responsibility	Intellect Sheath	Through Rin and Dharma
7.	Integrity	Intellect Sheath	Through working out personal dharma
8.	Intimacy	Self	Desire to connect that is manifested as an urge to love and be loved
9.	Integrating Adult	Strengthened Intellect Sheath; also the gateway to spiritual practice leading to Self-realisation	Can lead to connectedness with the Supreme Principle
10.	Physis and Aspiration Arrow of Script Matrix	Self	Longing to merge with Brahman (World Soul)

Dealing with Emotions

As mentioned earlier, there are four basic emotions: Anger, Fear, Sadness and Happiness, with several shades in between. We will not consider Happiness because according to *Vedanta* it is but a reflection of the inherent nature of the Self, which is Bliss.

It remains to deal with Anger, Fear and Sadness. Now anger is essentially a thwarted desire. When we want something and can't get it, we express our frustration by becoming angry. We can also become angry when we are not in a state of tranquillity and mental equilibrium.

The Vedantic way of dealing with anger is accordingly twofold: immediate action and long-term action.

Immediate Action: Detachment

> *"Like two golden birds perched on the selfsame tree, intimate friends, the ego and the Self, dwell in the same body. The former eats the sour and sweet fruits of the tree of life, while the latter looks on in detachment".*
>
> —*Mundaka Upanishad*

Here, of course, "ego" means the consciousness of oneself as an individual (a mental construct) and has nothing to do with the ego states of TA.

We have previously discussed the Vedantic way of becoming a witness to one's own anger as a way of conquering it. Luckily, the human being is endowed with a fertile imagination; it is possible to imagine oneself stepping out of one's body and observing it. Detachment creates distance, and distance lends a sense of perspective. Anger is an emotion intimately tied to the "I" consciousness, the sense of the personality. When we visualise ourselves "stepping away" from this sense, we cease our anger. For example,

Who is angry? I am angry, as a person. But I have a Self inside that person. Can I retreat into that Self and watch myself as a person being angry? Will I then remain angry?

As a matter of fact, detachment can help us in other circumstances also, as in the example of Dr. Victor Frankl quoted earlier.

Long-Term Action: Mindfulness and Meditation

Mindfulness is the practice of being fully alive to the present moment, in the here and now, (awareness in TA literature, a key component of autonomy) while passively observing the thoughts running through the mind. And the mind is like a chattering monkey, leaping from one thought to the other. To discipline it calls for willpower, concentration and effort. In fact, mindfulness is used as a prelude to meditation, which is essentially trying to still the mind and think of nothing at all. By doing so successfully, according to *Vedanta,* the Self begins to reveal Itself.

Advanced meditation techniques are practised by the yogis who have chosen to delve deeper into spirituality; however, it can be performed by the layperson also. (This includes me; I have been attempting meditation for years). There are several guided meditation techniques available on the Internet and elsewhere. My personal experience is that, although the revelation has not occurred in my case as yet, I get a wonderful sense of calmness, equanimity and detachment through my efforts at daily meditation. This helps tremendously in keeping me on an even keel. And it doesn't matter whether the revelation occurs or not, as with life, *the journey is the destination.*

Time to Learn

A young but earnest Zen student approached his teacher and asked him, "If I work very hard and diligently, how long will it take me to become a Zen Master?"

The teacher thought about this and then replied, "Ten years".

The student then said, "But what if I work very, very hard and really apply myself to learn fast—How long then?"

Replied the Master, "Well, twenty years".

"But if I really, really work at it. How long then?" asked the student.

"Thirty years", replied the Master.

"But, I do not understand", said the disappointed student, "Each time I say I will work harder, you say that it will take me longer. Why do you say that?"

Replied the Master, "When you have one eye on the reward, you have only one eye on the path".

Fear is of two kinds: that which arises due to clear and present danger to life and limb, and that which is illogical and unjustified. Our brains are "hardwired" for the former since the hunter-gatherer days, when it was a struggle simply to stay alive, but the latter can be merely ephemeral, a creation of the mind, born out of a sense of insecurity. In case of danger, the fight-or-flight response is automatic and unthinking but in the latter case, fear breeds worry that further breeds more fear, and so on.

In such cases, the intellect can come to our rescue. It makes sense to examine our fears and determine whether they are groundless or justified, and decide to either dismiss them or take appropriate action.

In this case too the equanimity resulting from mindfulness and meditation helps:

The Champion Archer

After winning several archery contests, the young and rather boastful champion challenged a Zen master who was renowned for his skill as an archer. The young man demonstrated remarkable proficiency when he hit a distant bull's-eye on his first try, and then split the arrow with his second shot.

"There" he said to the old man, "See if you can match that!"

The master smiled at him and said, "Come with me". He led the young champion down a rocky path, until they came to a deep chasm spanned by a rather flimsy and shaky log.

Calmly stepping out onto the middle of the unsteady and certainly perilous bridge, the old master picked a faraway tree as a target, drew his bow and shot a clean direct hit.

"Now it is your turn", he said as he gracefully stepped back onto safe ground.

Staring with terror into the seemingly bottomless abyss, the young man could not force himself to step out on the log, much less shoot at a target.

"You have much skill with your bow", the master said, sensing the young man's predicament, "but you have little skill with the mind that lets loose the arrow".

Sadness likewise can be completely necessary, as for example on getting news of the death of a loved one. It is certainly important not to keep emotions bottled up when grieving. However, it can also be brought about by unnecessary brooding for no good reason, leading to depression. Again, detachment helps, and the intellect comes to the rescue: Is it justified? Can I do anything about it? How long do I wallow in misery? The world is as it is: and, after all, *"This too shall pass"*.

Dealing with Behaviour

So far, we have been talking about the internal world; but when we consider behaviour, we need to consider others' behaviour in addition to our own, which brings us to the need to engage with external reality (context) and other persons also. According to *Vedanta*, the Self is the same in all persons, and thus there is no difference between "You" and "I", but this is an abstraction, difficult to understand for the layperson, and more difficult still to have an effect on behaviour. In my opinion, a simpler principle such as **"I'm OK, You're OK"** is a better guide for the intellect, because it places emphasis on the fact that I deserve to be treated with as much respect as the other person and the differences between us also need to be honoured:

Different Drums and Different Drummers

If I do not want what you want, please try not to tell me that my want is wrong;

Or if I believe other than you, at least pause before you correct my view;

Or if my emotion is less than yours, or more, given the same circumstances, try not to ask me to feel more strongly or weakly;

Or yet if I act, or fail to act, in the manner of your design for action, let me be.

I do not, for the moment at least, ask you to understand me. That will come only when you are willing to give up changing me into a copy of you;

I may be your spouse, your parent, your offspring, your friend, or your colleague. If you will allow me any of my own wants, or emotions, or beliefs, or actions, then you open yourself, so that someday these ways of mine might not seem so wrong, and might finally appear to you as right for me. To put up with me is the first step to understanding me. Not that you embrace my ways as right for you but that you are no longer irritated or disappointed with me for my seeming waywardness.

And in understanding me you might come to prize my differences from you, and far from seeking to change me, preserve and even nurture those differences.

Poem by David Keirsey

In my experience, the golden rule in dealing with behaviour, one's own as well as others, is to allow time for the intellect to come into play to make a considered response instead of reacting. This, of course, amounts to rehashing the traditional wisdom of "*Think before you speak*". One can then decide the most appropriate thing to do; continue the interaction by replying from the appropriate ego state, stop the interaction by crossing the transaction (replying from an unexpected ego state) or simply withdraw:

Rohan: "Let's go for a drink after work. We're colleagues and we should get to know each other better".

Ramesh (after a pause): "That's a good idea. It'll be nice to relax and talk about things other than office".

Or,

Ramesh (after a pause): "Why don't you concentrate on the report that you need to finish?"

Or,

Ramesh (after a pause): "No thanks, I have to get home early".

In the first case, Ramesh's intellect decides to take up his colleague's offer as he likes the proposal. In the second case, he may have decided that he doesn't really like him and consciously cut the conversation short. In the third case, he politely declines as he may have decided to withdraw from the interaction altogether.

The Golden Rule, if I may call it that, is to pause:

Practise the Pause

Pause before judging. Pause before assuming. Pause before accusing. Pause whenever you're about to react harshly and you'll avoid doing and saying things you'll later regret.

—Lori Deschene, American author

The principle of scrutiny by the intellect also applies in the case of behaviour arising out of psychological rackets and harmful psychological games, in TA terminology. The intellect can consciously examine the rackety (artificial) feelings to probe whether they are in fact a cover for something else. Likewise, it can recognise a game-initiating approach and decide whether to play along and endure the consequences, or stop the player dead in his tracks with an unexpected reply, or walk away from the person altogether. (For a detailed examination of rackets and games, the interested reader can refer to my earlier book or any other introductory book on TA).

However, a question that arises is that the patterns of thought and feeling that give rise to rackets and games are deeply ingrained into our subconscious selves, and outside our awareness. How then can the intellect consciously examine them?

At this stage, it is appropriate to recall the work of the great Swiss psychologist Carl Jung (1875–1961) and his theory of **Individuation**. This refers to the lifelong process of integrating the conscious and subconscious minds to become one's complete self. According to Jung, through committed individuation, we combine disconnected elements of our psyche and unfold our unique potential. Among the methods posited for individuation are meditation and strategic self-reflection to foster self-knowledge and growth. However, it requires courage, sustained effort and the willingness to confront one's weaknesses.

The similarity between Individuation and the Integrating Adult is striking. When we combine it with the Vedantic Ego States Model, both are identified with the Intellect Sheath. Also recall that the methods for strengthening the Intellect Sheath include introspection and reflection, which lead inescapably to mindfulness, the prelude to meditation. This gives us a pretty complete picture of autonomy and connectedness in TA terms, always remembering that these are processes and not destinations.

Assuming that we are able to do this: it means that the intellect has recognised, that is, brought into conscious awareness, previously submerged aspects of our personality. As we have seen, ideally, the intellect operates on the Mental Impressions Sheath to pick up what it considers of value from the (subconscious) Parent and Child ego states, using as its yardsticks conscience, reason, judgement and discrimination, and through the exertion of willpower.

Another answer comes from neurochemistry, which deals with the architecture of the human brain; the mind and intellect in action, so to speak. There are three distinct areas of the brain that are involved in thoughts, feelings and behaviour. These are: the *Neocortex*, the seat of our conscious mind, our identity and higher brain functions. This is the brain's chief designer, allowing us to remember, learn, reason, plan, create, analyse, forecast and speculate. The *Limbic area* of the brain is the chemical or emotional brain. Briefly speaking, an experience creates a specific chemical cocktail corresponding to a particular emotion/feeling. The *Cerebellum* is the seat of the subconscious. It stores certain types of simple actions and skills, along with hardwired attitudes, conditioned behaviours, emotional reactions, repetitive actions, habits and unconscious reflexes.

In layperson's language, we can call the Neocortex the Thinking part of the brain, the Limbic area the Doing or Feeling part, and the Cerebellum the Being part.

(I am indebted to Dr. Joe Dispenza's excellent book, *Breaking the Habit of Being Yourself*, for the above succinct explanation).

Through strengthening of the intellect, one can create a new state of being that overrides what was previously stored in the subconscious. We recall that the intellect functions as an operator on the mind (Mental Impressions Sheath). What makes this possible in terms of brain studies is *Neuroplasticity*, the brain's incredible ability to reorganise and adapt by forming new neural connections throughout life even in late adulthood. Literally speaking, they can be rewired with targeted practices.

Dr. Dispenza gives the following example:

> "... *suppose you recently read a few thought-provoking books on compassion...you learned about the philosophy of compassion (through other people's experience, not yours)... intellectually, you know your stuff...your spouse calls to say that you've been invited to dinner with your mother-in-law...already you're thinking about how you have disliked her intensely since she hurt your feelings three years ago. Soon you've got a mental laundry list...you never liked her... when you're around her, you just want to jump up and leave.*
>
> *Still sitting in your car, you remember those books on the philosophy of compassion... it occurs to you, maybe if I try to apply what I read...I might have a new experience of my mother-in-law...You decide not to react to her with your typical set of automatic programs... you ask yourself, How do I not want to feel, and how am I not going to act, when I see her?... you're starting to unwire or prune away that old you from functioning as an identity...you ask yourself, How can I modify my behaviour, my actions and my reactions so my new experience leads to a new feeling? So you picture yourself greeting and hugging her... and complimenting her... as you mentally rehearse your new idea of self, you continue to install more neurological hardware (in effect, a new software program) when you actually begin to interact with your MIL... your brain captured the thought as the experience, and "upscaled" its grey matter to look as though the experience had already occurred.... Soon... you find yourself sitting at dinner, face to face with 'goodol' Mom'...you remember what you learned... you stay in the present moment, open your heart*

> *and really listen to what she is saying. You no longer hold her to her past...you modify your behaviour... thereby creating a new experience with your MIL. This activates the limbic brain to cook up a new blend of chemicals, which generates a new emotion... you truly start to feel compassion for her.... You had such a great feeling that day that it lingers... you connect compassion with your mother-in-law...your mind and body were working together. You* <u>*embodied*</u> *compassion".*
>
> —*Breaking the Habit of Being Yourself*

Let us spend some time on this example. Suppose I am the person in it. In terms of the Vedantic Ego States Model, my Intellect *operates* on the Adult memory of my reading on compassion, *decides* to apply it to my meeting with my MIL, imagines a new experience upon meeting her, which creates a new feeling in me. It again *decides* to override the earlier programmed behaviour when I meet her, and apply my new thinking to actually create that experience of compassion, affection and empathy towards her. This reinforces the feelings that I had earlier imagined (These feelings, in TA terms, are properly a part of the Nurturing Parent ego state), and we have a very warm and friendly interaction.

My thinking has, then, made me ignore my subconscious program and create a new feeling/experience that has resulted in a change in my behaviour towards my MIL (apart from earning me the gratitude of my wife!). Repeated sufficiently (possibly in different contexts), it is possible for this pattern to become "hardwired" into my subconscious, so that my natural state of being *is* compassion. I have progressed from *thinking* to *doing* to *being*, through willpower and the disciplined use of my mind, since the brain is nothing but the mind in action. This can also be considered as the Integrating Adult in action:

> *"...anyone functioning as an Adult should ideally exhibit three kinds of tendencies: personal attractiveness and responsiveness, objective data processing, and ethical responsibility, representing respectively archaeopsychic*

[Parent], neopsychic [Child] and exteropsychic [Adult] elements "integrated" ... This "integrated person is charming, etc., and courageous, etc., in his Adult state, whatever qualities he has or does not have in his Child and Parent ego states".

—Eric Berne, Transactional Analysis in Psychotherapy (words in square brackets added)

Therefore, a new state of being can come about through the forces of the intellect and the will.

The Power of the Will

Meditation, as we have seen, is a great way to control emotions, and achieve concentration, calmness and detachment. It also results in strengthening willpower, for forcing stillness of the senses and attempting to gradually withdraw them from the external world, stronger and stronger willpower is required. This helps immensely when we go back to dealing with life's ups and downs:

"...If you can force your heart and nerve and sinew
To serve your turn long after they are gone,
And so hold on when there is nothing in you
Except the Will which says to them: "Hold on!"
..If you can fill the unforgiving minute
With sixty seconds worth of distance run,
Yours is the Earth and everything that's in it,
And—which is more—you'll be a Man, my son!"

—'If' by Rudyard Kipling

Willpower is the last refuge of the Intellect Sheath. When all else fails, it keeps us going, and it can also motivate and inspire others, as the following story of the Aztec people shows:

The Great Fire and the Little Water

A long time ago there was a great fire in the forests that covered our Earth. People and animals started to run, trying to escape from the fire. Our brother Owl was running away when he noticed a small bird hurrying back and forth between the nearest river and the fire. He headed towards this small bird.

He noticed that it was our brother the Sparrow. He was running to the river, picking up small drops of water in his beak, then returning to the fire to throw that tiny bit of water on the flame. Owl approached Sparrow and yelled at him: "What are you doing, brother? Are you stupid? You are not going to achieve anything by doing this. You must run for your life!"

Sparrow stopped for a moment. Looking at Owl, he answered gravely, "I am trying to do the best with what I have".

It is remembered by our Grandparents that a long time ago the forests that covered our Earth were saved from a great fire by a small sparrow, an owl, and many other animals and people who got together to put out the fire.

Where does spirituality come into it? From the higher levels of the Intellect Sheath, where morality, ethics and will reside. Wisdom, conscience (the Categorical Imperative), *Rin, Dharma*—all these are our guideposts in making it easier for the intellect to reprogram the subconscious and create a new state of being. Recall that the quest for spirituality starts with the Intellect Sheath, and the Autonomy enabled by the Integrating Adult has been referred to as *"the open door to spirituality"*.

This is, however, an ideal to aspire to. If we were able to achieve individuation easily and integrate desirable states of being into our total personality with little effort, then most of us would be happy, well-adjusted persons, able to overcome life's vicissitudes with ease and grow to our full potential. We know, though, that this is not the case.

Contaminations from our subconscious selves may exist in the Adult, which can restrict our achievements, block our Physis and hinder proper Adult functioning. Decontaminating the Adult is a complex issue that involves not only examining our existing mental impressions in the Parent and Child ego states, but also the contents of our Cultural Parent. We will discuss this in the following chapter.

7
Clearing Out the Clutter

"For everyone...has a cave or a den of his own, which refracts and discolours the light of nature; owing either to his own proper and peculiar nature, or to... the authority of those he esteems or admires..."

—Francis Bacon, Novum Organum, c.16th CE

Decontaminating the Adult

What happens when the Adult is contaminated by the Parent? Prejudice rears its ugly head; opinions are perceived as facts and the person comes across as overbearing. Or, one is excessively ready to help, solicitous to the point of being irritating and tries to please everyone, ending up pleasing no one at all. Similarly, contamination by the Child can result in a person being excessively obedient to authority or being rebellious or withdrawing by nature or being inappropriately childlike, impulsive and emotional.

For successful decontamination, then, we have to subject our Parent and Child ego states to the scrutiny of the intellect. A good place to start is the Script Questionnaire given in Annexure I. Reflecting on the answers will provide clues about one's psyche, as well as the elements (thoughts, feelings and behaviour) that we would like to work on and change. It may also reveal the psychological messages that we have imbibed from our parents when we were young, and our adaptation to those messages, which form part of our unconscious plan for satisfying them (script).

Since it is far easier to change behaviour than it is to change thoughts and feelings, we start with behaviour first. For example,

I have this image of myself that I'm a shy person. When I go to a gathering where I do not know anyone, I grab a drink and then head for a corner or the wall, where I try to look inconspicuous, clutching my drink and avoiding anyone's gaze. My body language says "Stay away from me!" and if anyone does approach me, I answer them in monosyllables until they get fed up and move away. I have a pretty miserable time, and when I'm leaving, I think to myself, "I knew I shouldn't have gone! I'm shy by nature, and there's no use going to a place where I don't know anyone".

Reflecting on my self-image brings up a memory of overhearing my mother telling her friend, "Don't ask Priya to recite a poem or anything like that. She's shy by nature, and she won't do it".

Another time, when I wanted to say something at dinnertime, my father told me with a frown, "Don't interrupt! Children should be seen and not heard. Eat your food".

*Repeated instances like this gave me the message **"Don't Be Yourself"**, and I understood that if I wanted my parents to be happy with me, I had to be as inconspicuous as possible.*

However, I'm grown up now and I need to change this behaviour if I'm going to be successful in my marketing job, which involves a lot of networking. So, the next time I go to a meeting like this, I'm not going to be a wallflower.

In the next gathering, I head to a group of people and join them, taking part in the conversation, pleasantly chatting and making new acquaintances. As I leave, I think to myself, "Well, that wasn't so bad! Maybe I should do this more often".

What is important, I believe, is to *try a behaviour change first and then allow the intellect to reflect upon it.* If it has worked, the intellect will create its own imagined reality for the next time, and so on. Repeated often enough, in other contexts also, the change in behaviour can lead to a change in attitude in the way we perceive ourselves.

We have then changed our thoughts also. The limbic brain, in accordance with the directives from the neocortex, releases a new blend of chemicals into our nervous system that generates a new emotion; pleasurable anticipation in place of the earlier discomfort. We can, in this way, arrive at a *new state of "being"*, which takes root in place of the old one. It basically involves concentration, imagination and willpower, all resources of the Intellect Sheath.

The intellect also recognises childlike thoughts, feelings and behaviour for what they essentially are, childish, and takes a conscious decision to release them only when appropriate. The principle again is to pause before choosing the ego state to bring into play:

"Do not learn how to react. Learn how to respond".

—Gautama Buddha

The other aspect is to consciously decide to jettison the parts of the script that have lost their relevance or are outmoded or are holding us back from achieving our full potential. Some messages given to us when we were children are simply not pertinent any more in adult life, such as:

"Grown-ups know more than you"

"The real world is different"

"Study hard so that you get good marks"

Similarly, there are internalised messages that restrict us:

"Don't get close to people; you'll end up getting hurt"

"Don't waste time on idle thoughts; concentrate on your work instead"

"You'll never amount to anything"

The following story illustrates this:

Conditioning Young Elephants

When an elephant is a baby, it is tied with a chain to a strong tree. It keeps tugging and pulling the chain, in vain. A day comes when it realises that all the tugging and pulling will not help and it gives up, thinking that it cannot break away from the bond. It stops and stands still.

And when the baby elephant becomes the mighty giant elephant, he is tied with a weak rope to a small stake. The elephant could, with one tug, walk away free, but it goes nowhere because it has been conditioned to believe that it cannot break away. It believes that the rope can still hold it, so it never tries to break free.

Like the elephant, we can also go through life hanging on to a belief that we cannot do something, simply because we had failed at it before. We are also being held back by old beliefs and avoid trying something new because of a limiting belief about ourselves.

However, the good news is that change is possible. It involves an examination of the beliefs we have held since childhood, introspection and reflection to decide upon their relevance in the current scenario, and jettisoning those that are no longer relevant or are holding us back. Needless to say, all this is done through the operation of the Intellect Sheath in our Vedantic Ego States Model.

As mentioned earlier, the Script Questionnaire is a good place to start, because it forces introspection and is likely to reveal aspects of our personality, which we were not consciously aware of or which we ignored. It is lengthy, to be sure, but as the saying goes,

"How do you eat an elephant?"

"You cut it into bite-sized pieces"

We take it one bite at a time, and reflect on the answers we provide. Honesty, of course, is of the essence. If we are not being honest, we are only deluding ourselves. This is likely to open up new pathways to explore, and give us valuable perspectives about ourselves and the forces that have shaped our personality. The idea is to examine these with the help of our intellect, and take a conscious decision in each case: is it still relevant to my functioning as an Adult? If not, can I jettison it, or transform it in such a way that it does not hinder my functioning?

For example, we have Drivers in our personality, which are essentially how we learned to do things so as to get the approval of the "big people" when we were small, or to try and live up to their expectations. In times of stress, as Adults, we tend to lapse into these. Unfortunately, these are preprogrammed to fail (if you can achieve it, then it doesn't drive you anymore). These Drivers can, after identification and upon reflection, be turned into Allowers:

I have a Driver "Please others" in my own psyche, which I identified with the help of an instrument like the Script Questionnaire. Reflecting on this, I understood that it was indeed true. I had a hard time saying "No" to other people, especially my relatives, even when they asked me to do something I really did not want to do. Reflecting on this, I could see how many times I had come to grief on this account.

I (my intellect) made a conscious decision to learn how to politely say "No" when asked to do something I really did not want to do, even to my relatives. So my Driver became an Allower: "I give myself permission to say No politely when asked to do something I really don't want to do". At first, my relatives and friends were a bit puzzled by my change in behaviour, which seemed out of character to them but sooner than I thought, they accepted the new "me" and thought no more of it. In fact, one of them even told me later privately that she admired the new "me" who stuck to his guns and didn't cave into other people's wishes!

(For a detailed discussion of Drivers, and what you can do about them, the interested reader can refer to my earlier book *Winning Hearts and Minds: Transactional Analysis Simplified*).

I realise, of course, that it is easier to write this than to actually do it by yourself. In some cases, professional psychotherapeutic help may be necessary to "untangle the knots", so to speak, but I still urge readers to try for themselves. If I have attempted it on my own, so can you.

What about the Cultural Parent?

> *"When a young woman decides to marry the man of her own choice, it is the Cultural Parent who is uncomfortable and wants to stop her. When a child*

is prevented from going to school, and is asked to look after the younger children, the Cultural Parent smiles with satisfaction. When a wife is beaten by her husband, the punitive part of the Cultural Parent grimly approves, and both parties are caught in its grip. The Cultural Parent contains the conscious and unconscious boundaries of acceptable behaviour, whether or not what is acceptable is harmful or helpful to the individual".

—Pearl Drego, The Cultural Parent, TAJ 1983

However, it would be erroneous to assume that the Cultural Parent contains only negative influences. In the Indian context, for example, respect for elders is deeply ingrained into our psyche and senior citizens are given priority treatment. This is not unusual in itself; this preferential practice is the norm in many other countries also. But when the feeling of respect extends to condoning or overlooking minor transgressions also, then the Indian Cultural Parent is at work:

I was driving home from an errand and made a U-turn in a place where it was expressly forbidden. The road was clear and obeying would have meant taking a detour, so I did it. On the pavement, hidden behind a tree, was a traffic cop waiting there precisely to catch errant drivers like me. After my U-turn, he emerged and waved me to the side of the road. Dismayed, I obeyed, and mentally prepared myself for receiving a challan (ticket), a lecture and a fine.

He was young, probably in his twenties, and he looked at me reproachfully and said, "Why?"

I did my best to look penitent, and said, "The road was empty, and I would have had to make a detour otherwise..."

He hesitated, and then briskly said, "Uncle, because of your white hair, I'm letting you off this time. But don't do it again!"

Similarly, it is considered bad manners to touch a person with one's feet. It denotes a lack of respect, even contempt. If an Indian does it accidentally, the person, almost as a reflex action, usually touches her forehead and heart to signify obeisance to the soul (*Atman*) of the other person. This is also the Cultural Parent weighing in.

That said, let us frankly admit that there are several things wrong with the Cultural Parent that are prejudicial, unjust, biased and completely out of tune with the times. As mentioned earlier, it takes courage to examine the accretions of thought/feeling/behaviour in our Cultural Parent dispassionately, and willpower to discard those that the intellect judges to be not relevant any more.

Here I would like to examine two examples in detail, one peculiarly Indian and the other almost universal. These are the caste system and patriarchy.

The Caste System

The original hymn of the Rig Veda, the oldest of the Vedas, speaks of the *Brahmin (*priest*)* being born of the mouth of the primeval Man, the *Kshatriya* (warrior) from his arms, the *Vaishya* (trader) from his thighs, and the *Shudra* (labourer) from his feet. This was a fourfold division based probably on the occupations that were known at that time: the priest who prayed and conducted Vedic rituals, the warrior who fought in battle, the trader who supplied necessities, and the labourer who worked in the fields. Through the offices of organised religion, this fourfold division was later converted into the straitjacket of the caste system, so that the segregation by occupation became segregation by birth: a Brahmin's child was a Brahmin, a Kshatriya's offspring a Kshatriya, and so on. Divine sanction was used to justify this wholly unjustifiable premise. Even worse, a community among the *Shudras* was designated Untouchables, who were at the very bottom of the caste ladder; their very shadow was deemed to be "polluting" to the upper castes.

The original caste system later morphed into subcastes and *jati* (communities) and families bound together by complicated lineages called *gotra*. But the straitjacket remained and has taken deep roots in the Cultural Parent of the Indian psyche. Till today, transgressions of the caste hierarchy are viewed severely by much of Indian society, except for a tiny minority.

Social reformers in India have raised their voices against caste from the nineteenth century onwards. Swami Vivekananda declared:

> *"The caste system is opposed to the religion of the Vedanta. Caste is a social custom, and all our great preachers have tried to break it down. From Buddhism downwards, every sect has preached against caste, and every time it has only riveted the chains..."*
>
> —*Speech at the Twentieth Century Club, Boston, USA*

The following story is also told about him:

Swamiji once spent a few days at a railway station in Rajasthan. People kept coming to him all day long with all sorts of questions, mostly religious, and he patiently answered everyone. Three days and three nights passed in this manner, and he was so engrossed in talking about spiritual matters that he did not even stop to eat, and the people who kept flocking to him never once thought of asking him if he had eaten.

On the third night, a cobbler who worked at the station approached him and said hesitantly, "Swamiji, I have watched you talking and talking for three days now, and you have not eaten even one morsel of food".

Swami Vivekananda looked at him and said, "Will you please give me something to eat?" The cobbler said, "I would very much like to, but I am of humble birth, not allowed to serve such as you. If you permit, I will bring you the ingredients, and you can prepare them".

Swamiji said, "No, my child, give me the food you have prepared. I will be happy to eat it". Overjoyed, the cobbler rushed to his hut and returned with freshly prepared food, which Swamiji consumed with relish.

In the meantime, some gentlemen came to visit the Swami and found he was eating food given to him by a cobbler. They came to him and protested that it was improper for him to accept food from one such. Swamiji heard them out and then said:

"You people made me talk without respite for the last three days, but you did not even care to inquire whether I had taken any food and rest. You claim you are gentlemen and boast of your high birth; what is more shameful, you condemn this man for being of humble birth. Can you overlook the humanity he has just shown and despise him without feeling ashamed?"

It is beyond the scope of this book to speculate how division by occupation turned into segregation by birth. Some historians are of the view that Brahmins wanted to preserve their supremacy and that of organised Hindu religion in the face of the rise of Buddhism and Jainism, which threatened the established social order. They wanted to be the sole repositories of knowledge, wisdom and access to God, and so they devised the straitjacket that would forever bind the *non-Brahmins*. In fact, an early Hindu religious text prescribes severe penalties for a Shudra who dares to even listen to the *Vedas*!

The pomposity of those who thought learning was their exclusive prerogative at times drew the gentle ridicule of spiritual teachers. Ramakrishna Paramhansa, beloved Master of Swami Vivekananda, was fond of telling the following story to his disciples:

The Learned Pandit

One day, several men were being ferried across a river. Among them was a pandit (priest), who was very proud of his knowledge and his understanding of the scriptures. As they were crossing the river, he looked around disdainfully at the villagers who were his co-passengers and decided to talk to them just to pass the time. He turned to the nearest man and said:

"I am a scholar. I have made a deep study of the Upanishads. Have you read the Upanishads?"

The simple fellow said, "No sir, I haven't".

"You poor fellow! A quarter of your life has been wasted. You must have read the Shastras then".

"No sir, I can't say that I have".

The pandit looked at him pityingly, "Then half your life is gone! What about the six systems of philosophy?"

"I'm afraid I haven't even heard of them, sir".

"Not heard of them! Then three-fourths of your life... Hey! What's happening to the boat?"

A sudden storm had arisen, and swept over them. The boatman cried out, "I'm losing control! Everyone jump overboard and swim to the shore!"

The villager shouted to the pandit, "Good sir, I hope you know how to swim".

The pandit stammered, "N-no! I never learned!"

"Never learned swimming? Then your whole life is gone, O panditji!" the villager shouted as he dived overboard.

The above was in a lighter vein; but to return to the reality, caste is a pernicious feature of Hindu society that persists to this day, in spite of many voices being raised against it time and again. Caste discrimination is also prohibited by law, yet it continues to rear its ugly head. In my opinion, we have our Cultural Parent to thank for this wholly unfounded practice that has been cloaked in religious trappings. The question of eradicating caste discrimination from Indian society is a complex one, which we will not discuss here; suffice it to say that it is necessary to cleanse this contamination from our Adult as individuals through the application of the intellect and the resources at its command. As Mahatma Gandhi said,

"Be the change that you want to see in the world"

For instance, I can:

- Express myself openly against caste discrimination.
- Acknowledge instinctive biases against caste and call out prejudices for what they are.
- Decide not to obey caste barriers on a personal level.

Patriarchy

In my opinion, this also has to do with the Cultural Parent. "It's a man's world" is a slogan that has been handed down to us over the centuries in all cultures. The man is universally seen to be the provider while the woman is seen as the caregiver who looks after home and hearth and bears and raises children, although recent anthropological discoveries suggest that women were hunter-gatherers alongside men, in addition to performing the above roles. However, the social system almost universally came to be set up in such a way that men held all the power and women were largely excluded from it. Women were under male domination, limited in their human rights, and subject to exploitation and discrimination. Wives have been regarded as chattels or possessions of the husband; women were not allowed to vote in the much-vaunted democracy of Ancient Greece; kidnapping a woman is recognized as a legitimate form of marriage in our scriptures; domestic violence against women has been a cruel historical fact, as witness the grim rhyme from Medieval England::

"A dog, a wife, and a walnut tree;
The more you beat them the better they be"

—Anon.

The problem was compounded by the fact that various cultures treated women as merely adjuncts to men; Eve was supposedly born from Adam's rib, and was cast in the role of temptress in Christian mythology. Women led men astray from their noble endeavours: Napoleon Bonaparte famously said:

"Love [of a woman] is the occupation of the idle man, the amusement of a busy one, and the shipwreck of a sovereign".

(Words in square brackets added)

With such influences being passed down the centuries and generations, patriarchy has unfortunately become hidebound in the Cultural Parent, which is reflected in society worldwide. However, there has been a pushback from feminists and the LGBTQ+ community that is gathering strength; a most welcome development. Very recently, thousands of women in Iceland went on strike in offices, hospitals, schools and homes, demanding an end to all forms of gender discrimination. They were also joined by the Prime Minister, Katrin Jakobsdóttir!

How do we, as thinking and perceptive adults, deal with this inbuilt bias? Once we recognise that the problem exists, it's again up to the intellect and its resources to tackle it. For instance, my Adult might:

- Start a conversation on gender equality and question existing discriminatory opinions and behaviours.
- Acknowledge errors in habitual patterns of thinking. (I have quoted my own example earlier, when I wrote something discriminatory and modified it when the stereotype was pointed out).
- Make a conscious and purposeful decision to change when confronted by my own patriarchal biases.
- Respect and encourage those who wish to break out of gender stereotypes.
- Question and defy regressive and discriminatory customs. I recognise that it is much easier to write about this than to do it, but on an individual level, it is surely possible. Change, after all, starts at the individual level, as pointed out by Mahatma Gandhi earlier. The following story also bears witness to this:

Making a Difference

An old man who lived near the sea had a habit of strolling along the beach early every morning. One day while out for his walk, he noticed a young girl walking along the coastline some distance ahead of him. She was frequently stooping, picking up something and throwing it into the sea.

His curiosity aroused, he hurried after her, and when he got near, he saw what she was doing. The tide had washed up several starfish on the beach, and she was picking them up and throwing them back into the sea.

He asked, "What are you doing, my dear?"

She said, "When the sun comes up, they'll die. I'm throwing them back so that they may live".

"But there are miles of coastline and thousands of starfish! What difference can your effort possibly make?"

She picked up another starfish and threw it back in the sea. Smiling at him, she said,

"Well, it sure made a difference to that one".

There does not appear to be any generalised way of uncovering and dealing with the contaminations in the Adult, since they are different for different individuals. However, in general, we can say that once we get an indication of what they are, we can tackle them by the application of the intellect, the willingness to be open minded, the courage to acknowledge problems and the willpower to deal with them. All these are however properties of the Intellect Sheath in our Vedantic Ego States Model. We have also earlier referred to Neuroplasticity, the wonderful property of the brain to rewire itself to create "a new state of being". And so, I believe it would be possible; the first step to "clearing out the clutter" is to use the resources of the Intellect Sheath to call out

- Prejudice
- Intolerance
- Bigotry
- Injustice
- Discrimination
- Apathy
- Insecurity

in *ourselves.*

If even one person breathes easier because we have spoken out, our effort is worthwhile. To that extent, our negative Cultural Parent is diminished and our Adult is decontaminated.

"The world will not be destroyed by those who do evil, but by those who watch them and do nothing."

—*Albert Einstein*

Annexure I

Personal Life—Script Questionnaire

Directions: Write a concise answer to each question. Attempt to give your initial response and then later go over all the questions with more reflection.

1. How did you see yourself as a child?

   ____

2. What is one important early decision you made as a child?

   ____

3. What are some of the main "dos" that you have learned and accepted?

   ____

4. What were some of the main "don'ts" that were programmed into you?

   ____

5. What manipulative games did you play as an adolescent to get what you wanted?

   ____

6. What were the pay-offs (rewards) of those manipulative games?

   ____

7. How did you see yourself as an adolescent?

   ____

8. How do you see your mother?

   ____

9. How are you like your mother?

   ____

10. How are you unlike your mother?

    ____

11. What does your mother say when she compliments you?

    ____

12. What does your mother say when she criticises you?

    ____

13. What is her main advice to you?

    ____

14. What could you do to make her happy?

    ____

15. What could you do to disappoint her?

    ____

16. What did your mother tell you (either directly or indirectly) about

    Life? ______________________________

    Death? ______________________________

    Love? ______________________________

    Sex? ______________________________

    Marriage? ______________________________

    Men? ______________________________

    Women? ______________________________

    Your birth? ______________________________

17. What do you wish your mother had done differently?

    ____

18. How do you see your father?

    ____

19. How are you like your father?

    ____

20. How are you unlike your father?

    ____

21. What does your father say when he compliments you?

    ____

22. What does your father say when he criticises you?

    ____

23. What is his main advice to you?

    ____

24. What could you do to disappoint him?

    ____

25. What did your father tell you (either directly or indirectly) about
    Life? ____________________
    Death? ____________________
    Love? ____________________
    Sex? ____________________
    Marriage? ____________________
    Men? ____________________
    Women? ____________________
    Your birth? ____________________
26. What do you wish your father had done differently?

    ____
27. What do you most like about yourself?

    ____
28. How do you see yourself now?

    ____
29. What are three things you'd most like to change about yourself?

    ____
30. What has been preventing you from changing those things?

    ____
31. Are you your "Own person" or are you living up to others expectations of what you "should" be?

    ____
32. What is one early decision you made about yourself that you feel you have since changed by making a new decision?

    ____
33. What do you most like about yourself?

    ____
34. What do you least like about yourself?

    ____

35. What games do you still play?
____

36. How did you see yourself five years ago?
____

37. How would you like to see yourself five years from now?
____

38. What are you doing now to make that ideal become real?
____

39. If you were to write your own epitaph. What would it say? _______________

40. What words do you fear might appear in your obituary?
____

41. What do you most want out of life?
____

42. If you could have three wishes, what would they be?
____

43. What was a critical turning point in your life?
____

44. When do you feel most "alive?"
____

45. When do you feel okay about yourself?
____

46. When do you feel not okay about yourself?
____

47. When was the best time or period in your life?
____

48. What kinds of risks have you taken lately?
____

49. When you give up games you play now, what do you suppose it will be like?
____

50. What is one new decision you would like to make?
____

51. What kind of new script will you write for yourself?
____

8
Tightening the Grip

"We are what we repeatedly do.
Excellence, then, is not an act but a habit."

—Aristotle, c. 4th century BCE

Just Do It

The above tagline for Nike, the sportswear company, actually has profound psychological and philosophical implications, if we examine it closely. In Greek mythology, Nike was the goddess of victory and was closely associated with Athena, goddess of wisdom and war, and Zeus, king of the gods. She is sometimes depicted as their divine charioteer, even as the intellect, in *Vedanta*, is depicted as the charioteer of the soul, and Lord Krishna, in the *Mahabharata*, assumes the role of the charioteer of the warrior Arjuna.

We have earlier discussed the TA strategy of breaking out of the self-reinforcing cycle of rackets (limiting beliefs about ourselves) by *consciously deciding to change our behaviour* the next time around. Also recall *Neuroplasticity*, the wonderful property of the brain (intellect) to rewire itself to create "a new way of being" or a new habit. Taken together, the implication is that if we decide to repeat the new behaviour sufficient number of times, *it becomes a new habit* in place of the old one.

In this connection, it is instructive to go through the following excerpts from a lecture on "Habit: Your Master or Your Slave?" by a disciple of the *Yogoda Satsang* Society/Self-Realisation Fellowship (YSS/SRF) of India, which was founded by ParamahansaYogananda:

> *"...Once you decide that you want to change, the best way to do it is to start small, bit by bit... and the biggest obstacle to changing is waiting for the internal motivation to change... just get started... we don't need motivation to brush our teeth every day...when we realise that habits do not depend on motivation, we realise that change is much easier than we might have previously experienced... bad habits cannot be stopped by merely wanting to eradicate them, but by reconditioning ourselves physiologically and psychologically with contravening good habits. Willingness is not enough; we must act, not once or a few times, but repeatedly and continuously, until the opposite good habit is installed.... We make too much of feelings... what does it matter how you feel? Act rightly, and in due course of time, the right feeling will come...*
>
> *—Talk by Swami Govindananda Giri at SRF Hollywood Temple, Jan. 2023*

In fact, the emphasis on right action is a constant theme throughout the Vedantic philosophical system. *Karma* is all about right action; in the *Mahabharata,* Lord Krishna exhorts an Arjuna despondent at the thought of fighting his brothers, to take up his arms as he is on the side of *Dharma.* Swami Vivekananda gives a clarion call to work tirelessly in a spirit of worship, without thinking of the results. This principle applies equally to trying to replace bad habits with good ones, and striving for personal growth and self-development.

It is instructive to read what a well-known management educator and leadership coach has to say about the philosophy of "Doing":

> *"We plan. We decide. We think. But we don't take action. Have you decided to lose weight? Yes? And you are probably wondering why you haven't lost weight although you decided three months ago. Success in life comes not from deciding to do things—but from doing them. Results are born out of action, not intent... We*

> *could all benefit by building a strong bias for action. Become someone who doesn't just think about it or talk about it—but does it."*
>
> *—Prakash Iyer, former MD, Kimberley Clark Lever*

When we "just do it", having first determined what it is about ourselves that we would like to get rid of or change or improve then *the change in behaviour leads the intellect to reflect upon it subsequently.* If we decide it is worthwhile and enjoyable, then we decide to repeat it next time around. And, in neurological terms, the limbic system of the brain releases a new blend of chemicals into our system to make us feel good about it.

Therefore, in order to pursue self-improvement, *Vedanta* exhorts us to:

- Decide the right action (think)
- Act rightly (behave)
- Reflect (think)

And not worry about feelings, which will follow.

In the above talk, Swami Govindananda also shares his own method, in the context of working on replacing bad habits (behaviour) with good ones. In short, it can be described as follows:

> *I tend to react in a particular way in a given situation. I know this kind of reaction is unhealthy for me; it's a bad habit. I decide that the first time in the day this situation occurs, I will respond in the opposite way; the good habit. However, I give myself permission to react in line with the bad habit in all subsequent situations of this type that may arise during the day. And I find that once I've said to myself, "No, I'm not going to react that way" in the beginning, <u>then I introspect</u> <u>on my decision</u> and find that it was the right decision, and it made me feel good to not react as usual. And later in the day, when that situation arises again, I don't need to make use of the permission, and am able to react the way I did the first time.*

This is, of course, how *he* does it; but in general, the principle is to apply the Intellect Sheath and use its faculties of discrimination, reasoning and judgement, together with the sense of morality and ethics to determine the best way forward, and to draw upon one's innate willpower to make the effort to proceed suitably. Indeed, it holds true in all situations in life.

Love What You Do

In business circles, there has been a lot of interest in design theory. This has been taken up by management educators and fashioned into a theory for "Designing Your Life" based on the premise that the perfect life (career) is out there waiting for you, and you just have to find it. Professors at the Design Lab of the Business School of Stanford University, USA, conduct a course called Designing Your Life, which is usually full shortly after being notified. They offer very good practical advice about creating a "dashboard" for yourself, trying out various options that make you feel good, talking to experts in different areas to determine your own interests, doing pilot projects in the chosen fields, etc., before finally settling down to the perfect career and the perfect life.

Unfortunately, it's not that simple. Life is messy, complicated, full of unexpected twists and turns and can be impacted by seemingly random events. We do not have data to determine how many of the hundreds of students who have done the Life Design course have actually achieved the perfect life: but the principle being advocated is clearly **"Do What You Love".** Common sense indicates that in our time on this planet, there are only a very few fortunate people who are actually able to do what they love and make a living out of it. And we know that life just happens while we are making plans. It doesn't give you everything in order; all it throws at you is a mess. That is *Maya*. It's your positivity and creativity that bring harmony and order into it.

Vedanta offers us the way out for ordinary folk who are not able to do what they love; it exhorts us to **"Love What You Do".** If I do my work, whatever it may be, *in a spirit of service to people,* considering that somewhere, somehow, it is benefiting somebody, I will be able to better appreciate my work; and yes, even enjoy it. My intellect rationalizes that work to be my *Svadharma* (personal *dharma*), I do it to the best of my ability; the feeling of satisfaction, even delight, comes, and... I love what I do. This can also be considered as an expression of my Physis (urge to become better), and moving forward on the path of Self-actualization:

> *Some time ago, there was a newspaper article about a scooter-rickshaw driver in Bangalore, whose job consisted of ferrying passengers to their destination for a fare. He made up his mind that he would provide an experience for his passengers for total customer satisfaction. He decorated his passenger cabin, put new upholstery on the seat, hung curtains, provided piped music and an emergency light, and kept the current newspaper and a bottle of mineral water handy,*
>
> *It was really a pretty mundane job—driving people around—but in a spirit of service to his customers, he transformed it into an experience that they would remember—and they did. Apart from their accolades was the internal satisfaction that he was doing his best. And that was the fulfilment of his Svadharma.*

What if there is a conflict between my *Svadharma* and the *Sadharana Dharma* (common or usually practised *Dharma*)? The Sanskrit phrase below, used to describe *Jnana* Yoga, (yoga of knowledge), gives a clue:

> *"Nitya, Anitya, Vivek, Vichar"*
>
> *—Cf. Swami Parthasarathy, Vedanta Treatise*

Nitya means "eternal", *Anitya* "noneternal", *Vivek* "discrimination" and *Vichar* "reflection". Thus, reflection on the distinction between the eternal and the transient will help to guide me toward the correct action. Of course, it may be required to bring *all* the resources of the Intellect Sheath to bear along with uncovering the "clutter" in my Mental Impressions Sheath (see previous chapter). After recognizing and discounting prejudices, and doing introspection, and with adequate reflection, I will usually know what I should do.

Getting it Right

Swami Vivekananda has also given a very clear guideline, which has been quoted earlier, i.e., *that action to which the maximum amount of good attaches and the least amount of evil, is the right action. Also, we need to pay as much attention, if not more, to the means of action as the end of that action* (Chapter VI). In other words, the means must be fair, honest and equitable (remember, according to the law of *Karma*, these are good causes that will inevitably have good effects).

I personally make a mental list of pros and cons when faced with a dilemma, and go with the alternative that has the greatest number of positives. However, this is not the only way available to the intellect. Morality (the Categorical Imperative of Immanuel Kant) is another test that can be applied. Is my proposed course of action in harmony with my conscience?

Still, another yardstick is *Manav Dharma*, the *dharma* of common humanity (see Chapter V). *Manav Dharma* recognises that every human being carries the spark of the imperishable soul (*Atman*) within oneself, which in turn is a reflection of the World Soul (*Brahman*). The test of humanity, then, is the deeper test that we can apply to our decisions. Indeed, this test should, in my opinion, be regarded as the supreme test, even if it flies in the face of convention:

Carried Forward

Two monks, one old and the other young, were walking through the countryside on their way to their monastery. They came to a stream, at the edge of which a young girl was hesitating as she did not want to wade into the water and get her dress wet. The younger monk saw her and hastily averted his eyes, as they belonged to a very strict order that forbade them to so much as look at the opposite sex. The older monk walked straight up to her, picked her up in his arms, waded across the stream, and deposited her on the other side. Then he calmly continued on his way.

The younger monk, aghast at the older one's conduct, hurried to catch up with him, and they silently walked on, although inwardly he was seething with rage.

An hour passed, and then two, and three. Finally, he could contain himself no longer and burst out, "Reverend Father, you know very well that the rules of our order forbid us to even look at women. Yet, back there at the crossing, you actually picked up that girl in your arms and carried her across! What were you thinking?"

The old monk looked at the young man and said calmly, "I left that girl back there at the crossing. Why are you still carrying her?"

I have personally always cherished this Zen story because it encapsulates so many of the truths of *Vedanta:*

- Helping others in need is the highest religion.
- Work with a spirit of service.
- Work with detachment.

There cannot be a decent body of knowledge or a decent philosophy without humanity. *Vedanta* underscores this point through the maxim *"Vasudhaiva Kutumbakam"*, which we have referred to earlier (see Chapter V): the whole family of human beings is my family.

Mindfulness and Meditation

To use the metaphors of Paramahansa Yogananda, in the dark jungle of life there are many pitfalls; bad habits and moods. Once we get into them, we can't easily get out. As bad habits are harmful to our body and psyche, so moods are also harmful to the extent that they cloud our judgement and hamper clarity of thought. We have earlier explored working on changing bad habits, in the address of Swami Govindananda. As far as moods are concerned, daily practising mindfulness and meditation promotes even-mindedness, calmness and tranquillity.

Recall that TA also attaches great importance to mindfulness, regarding it as a key practice for the Adult to stay grounded in the here and now. However, according to the Vedantic Ego States Model, the Adult actually has two parts: *first*, the information and knowledge regarding external reality retained in the Mental Impressions Sheath, and *second,* the Intellect Sheath, with its resources of reasoning, judgement, discrimination, morality and willpower, which acts as an operator on the Sheath of Mental Impressions as well as interacting with external reality, and also picking up *what it considers appropriate* from Parent, Adult and Child, to determine how we will think, act and feel in any given situation. Beyond the Intellect Sheath lies the Bliss Sheath, enclosing the soul (*Atman*) that gives life to all the sheaths that make up the body-mind complex (including the Vital Air Sheath enclosing the Mental Impressions Sheath, and the outermost Food Sheath).

For calming the restless mind, then, we go beyond the Intellect Sheath and approach the stillness of the Bliss Sheath, where we simply observe all that is happening around us in the present moment in a detached manner. This is the essence of mindfulness.

To go beyond mindfulness, we practise meditation, which consists of trying to make the mind perfectly blank, and think of nothing at all. Various techniques are available for this, such as chanting a *mantra* (invocation) or concentrating on a candle flame, or trying to observe your breathing; but essentially, this is the idea.

Through rigorous and repeated meditation, the sages say, one can realise the Self (*Atman*) and thus God (*Brahman*). However, this is the way of the *Yogi* or spiritual seeker. For the vast majority of us, it is enough if we gain control over our feelings and impulses through the daily practice of meditation and recognise that the same *Atman* exists in all living beings. As a natural corollary to this, it follows that they need to be treated with compassion and respect.

Pranayama: Controlling the Emotions

We will now briefly discuss the Vital Air Sheath, which encloses the Mental Impressions Sheath. The Vital Air in Sanskrit is called *Prana* and refers to the subtle life force in the breath, which is the actual animating energy in the nervous system and the whole body:

Two Sages

Two sages lived in a hermitage in a forest. They spent most of their time worshipping Vayu, God of the Winds. One afternoon, as the sages were beginning their meal, a beggar arrived holding his begging bowl. He pleaded to the sages, "Pardon me, could I beg for a part of your meal?"

"Sorry, we cannot spare you any food", replied one of the sages. The persistent beggar continued, "May I ask you most humbly, which God do you worship?"

"We worship Vayu, the Wind God", answered one of the sages with pride, "He is also known as Prana, the breath of life".

"Ah! Then you must know that Prana pervades the whole universe", said the beggar. The sages were getting impatient, "Yes, yes, we know all that".

The beggar then asked, "O honourable sages, could you tell me to whom you made the food-offering?" "Prana, the life force, who else?" said the irritated sage. The beggar smiled and replied, "I am also a part of the universe. It is Prana, the life force, which pulsates in me, as this hungry body stands before you and speaks", appealed the beggar. The sages were trapped in the argument and admitted, "You speak the truth". The beggar then made his final appeal, "Then, in denying me food, you are denying Prana, for whom you have prepared the food".

The sages had no answer. Ashamed, they gladly shared their food with the beggar.

Since *Prana* is essentially an energy field, an emotion can be viewed as a current of energy generated by the mind (brain) and transmitted into the body through the nervous system. The visible manifestation of the energy field is breathing, and so controlling one's breathing will help to control this energy field. It follows that we can control, or at least influence, our emotions by practising breathing exercises specifically designed to soothe the emotions and calm the restless mind. These exercises are called *Pranayama*, and are an integral part of *Hatha* Yoga, the yoga of the body.

Of course, the discipline of *Hatha* Yoga has now morphed into many forms, including aerobic yoga, hot yoga, Iyengar yoga, Bikram yoga, Yin yoga, Power yoga and so on. All these have their own adherents and are no doubt very useful for bodily exercise. However, we are concerned with the specific set of breathing exercises (*Pranayama*) laid down in the ancient Indian scriptures, for bringing about tranquillity and even-mindedness. *The principle is to infuse life energy into the muscles by contracting them, pulling the currents of emotional energy into the breath, and then expel them from the body by releasing the breath.* The actual exercises can be found in any good book on yoga or can be performed with the help of an instructor.

Therefore, it is vitally important to make yogic exercises (including *pranayama*) and meditation part of one's daily routine, if we wish the charioteer to properly guide the horses through the unexpected twists and turns of the road more travelled, called Life.

The Role of Intuition

Indeed, meditation has another great benefit in everyday life; it refines the intellect to the point where flashes of intuition strike to show the correct way. Intuition has been called the *sixth sense*. It is that mysterious feeling you get when you "sense" the atmosphere in a room you enter, or you "sense" eyes boring into your back, or have a "gut feeling", or something "just feels right". However, it is not a sense at all, but rather your soul (*Atman*) giving you a gentle nudge through the Bliss Sheath.

According to the scriptures, the *Atman* is a silent witness to everything we do, our deeds and misdeeds, and I have referred to it as such; however, many great Yogic masters are of the opinion that the *Atman* sometimes expresses itself through our intuition, and meditation can develop the intellect up to this point:

> *"The important thing is to refine the power of reason until it becomes intuitive. Whenever you need correct thinking about a situation, calm yourself first. By*

> *meditation, go deep into the calm region of the soul; and as soon as you are aligned with your soul, inner vision and illumined understanding will come and you will be able to think correctly and find the right course in everything you do. Soul intuition is the light that can never make mistakes.*
>
> —*Paramhansa Yogananda, Yogoda Satsanga Annual Issue, 2023.*

Again:

Don't let the mind run constantly after your problem. Let it rest at times, for intuitive guidance often makes itself known through the loopholes between thoughts and emotions when the mind is calm....Intuition sees all, whereas reason sees only one thing at a time. Reason is a sort of ray that comes out of the light of intuition.

We have seen, in the cases of Kekule and Mendeleev (Chap. VI), how flashes of intuition guided both men to ground breaking discoveries, the former when he was asleep and the latter when he had laid his problem aside temporarily. It is also relevant to note that Dr. Eric Berne had spoken of discovering the foundations of TA intuitively. If we suppose the sense of identity (this is me, body, mind, likes, dislikes, warts and all) to be like a suit of armour that we put on about ourselves; this suit has chinks in it, through which the flashes of intuition can shine.

I was listening to "Anthem", a song by Leonard Cohen, the legendary Canadian singer-songwriter, while writing this. He is well known for his enigmatic lyrics, which are capable of diverse interpretations. Suddenly, the lyrics of the song made a lot of sense to me:

> *"Ring the bells that still can ring*
> *Forget your sacred offering*
> *There is a crack, a crack in everything*
> *That's how the light gets in".*
>
> —*Leonard Cohen*

I have no way of knowing what Cohen meant, since he has sadly passed; but I like to think it refers to the flashes of intuition that can illuminate the intellect at any time and at any place.

Opposing Forces

Another theme in *Vedanta* is that of opposing forces trying to gain control of the composite human personality. We have seen the allegory of the body as a chariot, the mind as the reins, and the intellect as the charioteer, in the *Katha Upanishad* (Chapter II). The verse goes on to describe the horses as the senses and selfish desires as the roads they travel. The soul, of course, is the traveller, seated in the chariot for the duration of its earthly existence.

This allegory has been amplified and interpreted to say:

> *"...there is a great tug of war going on between the senses and the soul. Each is trying to control the mind and intelligence. The senses pull the mind towards material gratifications, while the soul prompts the intelligence to direct the course of life wisely to achievement of higher goals".*
>
> *—Paramhansa Yogananda, Yogoda Satsang Annual Issue, 2023.*

The "tug of war" story is found in other cultures as well like the following Native American tale told many times around the Sacred Fire:

Wolves Within!

An old Grandfather, whose grandson came to him with anger at a schoolmate who had done him an injustice, said, "Let me tell you a story. I too at times have felt great hate for those that have taken so much, with no sorrow for what they do. But hate wears you down, and does not hurt your enemy. It is like taking poison and wishing your enemy would die. I have struggled with these feelings many times".

He continued, "It is as if there are two wolves inside me; one is good and does no harm. He lives in harmony with all around him and does not take offence when no offence is intended. He will only fight when it is right to do so, and in the right way".

"But the other wolf, ah! He is full of anger. The littlest thing will set him into a fit of temper. He fights everyone, all the time, for no reason. He cannot think because his anger and his hate are so great. It is hard to live with these two wolves within me, for both of them try to dominate my spirit".

The boy looked intently into his grandfather's eyes and asked, "Which one wins, Grandfather?"

The Grandfather solemnly said, "The one I feed".

Are we feeding the right wolf?

9
Confluence

"...science in its most advanced stage now is closer to Vedanta than ever before".

—Alfred North Whitehead, British mathematician and philosopher

The purpose of this chapter is to show how three streams of cutting-edge science, along with TA, are flowing inescapably towards the ocean of *Vedanta.* The sciences are Quantum Mechanics, Neurochemistry and Molecular Biology.

Quantum Mechanics

Physics is essentially a search for the laws of Nature; how the world and the universe which it is a part of, works. Quantum mechanics or wave mechanics is the new physics; an inquiry into the nature of matter, energy, space and time at the subatomic level. At first sight, it seems incongruous that physics should have anything to do with *Vedanta,* an inward-looking philosophy that deals with abstractions like the soul, the intellect and the mind, but that is far from the case.

Classical physics gave us a worldview that explained the workings of the universe satisfactorily till the end of the nineteenth century. However, as scientists probed deeper and deeper into Nature, aided by technological advances, it soon became apparent that the old laws of physics would not work at the level of the building blocks of matter: atoms. Ultimately, it was replaced by modern physics, which painted a very different picture of the world, one which had profound philosophical implications.

The new physics began in 1900 with the discovery of quantum theory by Max Planck, and the special theory of relativity by Albert Einstein. These theories revolutionised our ideas (and our experience) of matter, energy, space and time. Subsequently, Einstein worked out general relativity and a host of other illustrious physicists developed quantum mechanics, the most complete description of the world that we have to date. But it is not the world as we know it.

> *"In our endeavour to understand reality, we are somewhat like a man trying to understand the mechanism of a closed watch. He sees the face and the moving hands, even hears it ticking, but he has no way of opening the case...he may form some picture of a mechanism that could be responsible for all the things he observes, but he may never be quite sure his picture is the only one that could explain his observations. He will never be able to compare his picture with the real mechanism."*
>
> —*Albert Einstein*

It is extremely difficult to visualise the world unveiled by quantum mechanics because it runs completely counter to our normal experience. Moreover, it is impossible to say positively that this is the correct vision, or indeed the only possible vision.

Without going into details, these are some of the features of the universe uncovered by quantum mechanics:

- Every wave (of energy) has a particle (of matter) associated with it, and vice versa (de Broglie waves).
- It is impossible to accurately determine both the position and momentum of an object. If one is accurately determined, the other is indeterminate within a certain area (Heisenberg Uncertainty Principle).
- The act of observing something disturbs it. Before being observed, that "something" is actually an array of possibilities, which collapses into the discrete "something" when it is observed.
- Light can behave both as a wave and a particle (Wave Particle Duality).

- The separate parts of the universe are somehow connected in an intimate and immediate way (Bell's Theorem).
- List of particles inside the atom (at present): Proton, Electron, Neutron, Higgs boson, Neutrino, Up quark, Photon, Alpha particle, Pion, Bottom quark, Positron, Muon, Down quark, Strangeness quark, Tau, Antileptons and Antielectrons.

And that's not all. More than 200 subatomic particles have been detected, created by collisions in cosmic ray bombardments or in particle accelerators.

- Massive objects in the universe like the stars and planets create distortions in space-time, which results in gravitational forces and the "bending" of light.
- The universe is not a vast empty space as previously imagined, but a boiling, seething mass of galaxies and stars being born, exploding and dying to become "black holes" where the laws of physics do not apply. It is full of mysterious substances like antimatter and dark matter.

A favourite cartoon among physicists shows a lecturer addressing a convention of scientists:

> *"Along with antimatter and dark matter, we have discovered the existence of a third substance called "Doesn't Matter", which seems to have no effect on the universe whatsoever".*

Albert Einstein refused to believe that Nature could be left to randomness and indeterminacy. He famously said,

> *"God does not play dice with the Universe".*

He spent the final years of his life trying to reconcile quantum physics and relativity into a grand Unified Field Theory that would explain the complete workings of the universe. He could not do it; the search continues with theories of "strings" and "superstrings". But the more the physicists hunt, the more elusive the search becomes. At present, we can only say with Shakespeare:

> *"There are more things in Heaven and Earth, Horatio, than are dreamt of in your philosophy".*
>
> *—William Shakespeare, Hamlet: Prince of Denmark*

Implications

What can we say about all this, in the light of *Vedanta*?

The Vedantic Ego States Model recognises that the composite human being is made up of both matter and energy fields, inasmuch as the Food Sheath is matter, the Vital Air Sheath partly so, and the rest of the Sheaths are pure energy fields. So, of course, is the core or Self.

Further, as human beings, we cannot achieve absolute knowledge of anything. Whether we probe the smallest or the biggest phenomena in the universe, we are met with chaos, uncertainty, randomness and indeterminacy, and find ourselves further and further away from the grand unifying principles that we had hoped to find, that would explain the workings of Nature. We have no way of knowing whether the explanations so laboriously constructed are indeed correct or not.

Nature, of course, is a reflection of the Supreme Principle that has created the universe. *Vedanta* describes this Supreme Principle only as "*Neti, Neti*", that is, "*Not this, not that*".

Or, listen to the physicists themselves:

> *"The Fundamental Physics Group found it necessary.... To acknowledge that it might not be possible to construct a model of reality. This acknowledgment is more than recognition of the limitations of this theory or that theory. It is a recognition emerging throughout the West that knowledge itself is limited. Said another way, it is a recognition of the difference between knowledge and wisdom".*
>
> *—Gary Zukav, The Dancing Wu Li Masters: An Overview of the New Physics*

Again,

> *A vital aspect of the enlightened state is the experience of an all-pervading unity. "This" and "That" are no*

> *longer separate entities. They are different forms of the same thing. Everything is a manifestation. It is not possible to answer the question, "Manifestation of what?" because the "what" is that which is beyond words, beyond concept, beyond form, beyond even space and time. Everything is a manifestation of that which is. That which is,* **is.** *Beyond these words lies the experience of that which is.*
>
> —Ibid.

Also, quantum mechanics tells us that both observer and observed are joined together at the hip, that is, one is meaningless without the other. In other words, the frame of reference has to be the same for both, for the world to work properly. And if all separate parts of the universe are connected, as Bell's Theorem implies, then you, me and all of us, all living and nonliving things, the mountains, seas and forests, the universe are all connected. What else can connect them besides *Brahman*? And *Brahman,* as we know, is *Atman*, the Self. In the words of the poet,

> *"We're searching for something that has already found us".*
>
> *—Jim Morrison, An American Prayer*

Neurochemistry

The Bet

In 1998, neuroscientist Christof Koch bet philosopher David Chalmers that researchers would discover how the brain produces consciousness within 25 years, by 2023. The bet was for a case of wine. On 23rd June 2023, Koch owned up that he had lost and publicly handed over the case. Thereupon, Chalmers told him that he was angling for another case by 2048 because even by then science would not be able to solve this problem.

How do physical processes in the brain give rise to the subjective experience of the mind and the world? How does three-and-a-half pounds of grey matter containing 84 billion neurons firing in different combinations give rise to my sense of identity and my experience of the environment? We have hinted at this problem earlier in the imaginary dialogue between Socrates and Protagoras (Chapter IV). Neurochemistry cannot tell; it can only guess, with different theories competing for attention. However, suppose we take consciousness itself as a fundamental element of the world. In that case, the picture is quite different.

From *Vedanta,* we are told that one of the attributes of the Supreme Principle *Brahman* is *Chit,* Consciousness. Further, this consciousness is infused into the Self (*Atman*) at the core of the five sheaths (*Pancha Kosha*), because

"Atman is Brahman"

Change Your Brain, Change Your Life

> *"...people can literally change their brains and change their lives by... correcting negative beliefs and using meditative processes...In one series of studies we published, the practice of meditation... boosted blood flow to the prefrontal cortex, the most thoughtful part of the human brain. After eight weeks of daily meditation, the prefrontal cortex at rest was stronger, and the memories of our subjects were better, too".*
>
> *—Daniel G. Amen, M.D.*

We have earlier referred to *Breaking the Habit of Being Yourself* by Dr. Joe Dispenza (Chapter VI). The quotation above is taken from the Foreword to the same. It is quite instructive to peruse some of the other observations in Dr. Dispenza's book:

> *"... we unconsciously live by a set of memorised behaviours, thoughts, and emotional reactions, all running like computer programmes behind the scenes of our conscious awareness. [It is necessary to] enter into the operating system of the subconscious mind and make permanent changes where those programmes exist".*
>
> *(Words in square brackets added)*

Here we have corroboration from neurochemistry of the foundational (intuitive) premises of TA, and an acknowledgement that it is possible to change this. Further,

> *"...we have a natural ability to change the brain and body by thought alone... Because you can make thought more real than anything else, you can change who you are from brain cell to gene".*

This in turn is an acknowledgement of the power of the intellect in the Vedantic Ego States Model. Continuing,

> *"... you have three "brains" that allow you to move from thinking to doing to being...when you focus your attention to the exclusion of your environment, your body and time, [meditation] you can easily move from thinking to being without having to do anything.... [you will start] rewriting your automatic habits, attitudes, and other unwanted subconscious programmes".*
>
> *(Words in square brackets added)*

This is at once an expression of the Vedantic practice of meditation, the ability of the intellect to introspect and reflect, and an acknowledgement that we can move towards autonomy. Further,

> *"... your brain changes electromagnetically when you are focused ... the true purpose of meditation is to get beyond the analytical mind and enter into the subconscious mind so you can make real and permanent changes [in your personality]".*
>
> *(Words in square brackets added)*

Vedanta of course goes further; the true purpose of meditation is to connect with something greater than ourselves, to connect the Soul with the World-Soul, to realise that *Atman* is *Brahman*; but it is instructive to see Science getting closer and closer to Philosophy.

Molecular Biology

Epigenetics

Epigenetics literally means "control over genetics". It is a revolutionary field in molecular biology established at the beginning of the millennium, which profoundly changes our understanding of how life is controlled. It was earlier thought that the replicating mechanism of living cells (how they multiply) is controlled by its DNA, which represents the cell's long-term memory, passed on from generation to generation. However, Epigenetics shows that environmental signals control the activity of regulatory proteins that direct the activity of the DNA. In simplified terms, what this means is that *DNA does not control biology; a living cell's operations are primarily shaped by the environment it is in, not its genetic code.* Further, Epigenetics has determined that the "brain" of a cell is not its nucleus, as previously thought, but the membrane that covers it.

What has this to do with TA and *Vedanta*? The following quote is revealing:

> *"...the lessons of the Magical Membrane... put the control of our lives not in the genetic roll of the dice at conception but in our own hands. We are the drivers of our own biology..."*
>
> —*Dr. Bruce Lipton, The Biology of Belief*

Further,

> *"Learning how to harness your mind to promote growth is the secret of life...teachers like Buddha and Jesus have been telling us the same story for millennia. Now science is pointing us in the same direction. It is not our genes but our beliefs that control our lives..."*

Self-limiting beliefs and imaginary fears produce stress, which impacts the body and mind negatively; the molecular biologist poses a question:

> *"Because holding on to our fears and our pain is a fundamental, underlying determinant for chronic stress behaviours, is it possible that love, the polar*

opposite of fear, could be an antidote for stress and its related diseases?"

In Chapter IV, we have extensively discussed the Vedantic view that love is an "intense longing on the part of two to become one, and, after all, it may be, of all to become merged in one" (Swami Vivekananda) and also the TA view that love is essentially a sense of "connectedness" which has a spiritual dimension (Cook). According to Epigenetics, it turns out that love also heals the body and the mind:

"A lifetime without Love is of no account

Love is the Water of Life

Drink it down with heart and soul"

—Jalaluddin Rumi, Sufi poet, c.13th century AD

Conscious Parenting

Here is my challenge to you [parents]. Let go of unfounded fears and take care not to implant unnecessary fears and limiting beliefs in your children's subconscious minds. Most of all, do not accept the fatalistic message of genetic determinism. You can help your children reach their potential and you can change your personal life. You are not "stuck" with your genes.

This sounds very much like something a TA counsellor would say or something you would read in the pages of the Transactional Analysis Journal!

Further,

"Abusive developmental experiences specifically program a child's subconscious mind with vital protection behaviours to cope with life in a dangerous world. These programmed responses... ensure short-term survival".

The body, broadly speaking, has two systems necessary for its maintenance and development: a protection system and a growth system. In layman's language, the more the protection system kicks in, the more the growth system gets repressed, inhibiting development up to true potential. In The Biology of Belief, Dr. Lipton makes the point that:

> *"Each of us must stop to consider how negative programming impacts children's futures, for we are helping to shape the fate of human civilization".*

Spirit and Science

> *"...the latest discoveries in physics and cell research are forging new links between the worlds of Science and Spirit...I truly believe that only when Spirit and Science are reunited will we be afforded the means to create a better world".*

The Vedantic Ego States Model combines spirituality and psychology to go beyond the outer trappings of personality and show the inmost essence of the human being. It offers valuable insights as to how we can use our Intellect Sheath to become better human beings and live in harmony with those around us and with Nature. We *are*, in a way, speaking of a combination of spirituality and (social) science. Dare I imagine that knowledge and application of this model will play a part in creating a better world?

We are Manifestations of the Supreme Principle

Dr. Lipton goes on to say:

> *"Consider the human body as a television set. You are the image on the screen. But your image did not come from inside the television. Your identity is an environmental broadcast that was received via an antenna. One day you turn on the TV and the picture tube is dead..... But did the image die along with the set?.... You get another television set, plug it in, turn it on and tune it to the station... the broadcast image is still on the air, even though your first television "died"... the death... in no way killed the identity broadcast that comes from the environment....my identity, my "self", exists in the environment whether my body is here or not".*

Again,

> *"... consider the possibility that an embryo in the future displays the same set of identity receptors that I now*

> *possess. That embryo will be turned into my "self". My identity is back but playing through a different body..."*

And finally:

> *"The environment represents "All That Is" (God) and our self-receptor antennas download only a narrow band of the whole spectrum, we all represent a small part of the whole... a small part of God".*

The Vedantic philosopher would add that the environment, and indeed the whole universe, is a manifestation of the Supreme Principle (*Brahman*), of whom the individual Self (*Atman*) is but a part.

Epilogue

In this book, I have tried to present some elements of *Vedanta* philosophy in a simplified form, relating them to TA concepts. The idea is to show how they provide illuminating insights into issues arising out of the spiritual dimensions of TA theory. I have also applied the ego states concept of TA to the *Pancha Kosha* (Five Sheaths) model of the composite human personality to develop a Vedantic Ego States Model, which describes in detail the workings of the Adult. Further, the judicious use of the Intellect Sheath together with the insights provided by *Vedanta* can help us think properly; get rid of unconscious harmful programming in our subconscious; provide us with a strong moral compass; erase redundant beliefs and avoid inappropriate behaviour. It can help us live with gratitude, for every time we repay our *Rin* (debt), this is what we are really doing. It can help us forge a deep connection with those close to us, and also foster a sense of humanity and enable us to live in harmony with our environment.

Self-Development and Personal Growth

Autonomy can be described as the freedom to think and act as the intellect (charioteer) directs. Encouragement to work out one's own moral and ethical code (*Svadharma*) in accordance with the responsibility of discharging *Rin* would mark the beginning of the process of achieving autonomy, and serve to make children learn to assume responsibility for their actions. Similarly, adults too can learn how the combination of Indian and Western streams of thought can bring fresh purpose into their lives. The five sheaths constituting body, mind and soul can be sensed through various exercises (Ref. www.yogainternational.com); strengthening them through the yoga techniques mentioned in Table 1.1 will result in sound physical and mental health. Observance of *Yama* and *Niyam*a prompts us to tread the path of ethics, morality and goodness (*Dharma*) and gives us a framework within which we can live and work. The *Purushartha* gives us concrete objectives towards which we can direct our efforts.

Using the Vedantic Ego States Model

Personally speaking, from the model, I learned:

- Not to accept anything until it is ratified by my intellect.
- To use my intellect to question old beliefs, attitudes and opinions, and discard what I determine is no longer relevant in my present context.
- To "practise the pause", and let my intellect decide the most appropriate actions and behaviour in all situations.
- To make simple yogic breathing exercises and meditation part of my daily routine.
- To give priority to actions over feelings.
- To practise detachment to control my feelings and impulses.
- To work with a spirit of service and detachment.
- To be guided by my intellect, my conscience and my intuition in all situations.
- To consider humanity as the supreme religion.
- To discharge my fivefold debts (*Rin*) to the extent possible.

It may be observed that no specialised training or study, apart from learning simple yogic breathing exercises, and a technique of meditation, is required for applying the model to oneself.

Also, the model and the insights of *Vedanta* philosophy will be useful to TA practitioners in all the fields of application:

Practice Implications: Psychotherapy

The objectives of TA psychotherapy include helping clients to become more autonomous and script-free, work towards the **I'm OK-You're OK** position, learn to state their needs and views clearly without game-playing and take responsibility for their own feelings. The therapist encourages them to think for themselves and shows them that they can change if they want to. The Vedantic conception that the 'thinking' part of the mind, that is, the intellect acts (operates) upon the rest of our mental constructs will, I believe, make it easier for the clients to change the way they think about things and help in decontaminating the Adult. Appreciation of the complex functioning of the intellect as elaborated in the previous chapters may enable truly autonomous functioning. Knowledge and application of the Vedantic principles, learning how to strengthen the Intellect Sheath, and working out one's *Svadharma*, would go a long way in making effective use of the Integrating Adult.

The therapist can support clients in their endeavour for spiritual enrichment, and guide them to practise yogic exercises and meditation, which are of proven effectiveness in tackling various psychosomatic conditions like stress, anxiety, depression, insomnia, etc., apart from promoting all-round health of the body and mind.

Counselling

The TA practitioner helps clients to identify and use their own resources in an attempt to change themselves. The practitioner encourages clients to explore alternate ways of behaving and to make new decisions about themselves, challenging **Not OK** positions they may have adopted in childhood and reconstructing their scripts to make them more positive. The Vedantic model of ego states will bring into sharp focus the resource of the Intellect Sheath as well as guide clients to bring about positive change in themselves. Usage of this resource with encouragement and guidance of the counsellor will, with practice and time, serve to clear contaminations of the client's Adult, and lead the client progressively towards autonomy. For example, the contracting process in counselling or psychotherapy can be viewed in terms of using the (discriminating) intellect to identify specific behaviours and beliefs that the client desires to change. Subsequently, working jointly with the practitioner, the client can be guided to examine their own attitudes and behaviour, and decide what is of value and what is not through the use of discrimination and judgement functions of the intellect (in the Vedantic sense). The decision (or redecision) to jettison an old belief is similarly made through the functioning of the intellect (cf. Swami Rama, quoted earlier).

The spirituality inherent in the Vedantic conception of the personality also serves to connect with a higher purpose, and should be helpful in the case of clients battling with a sense of meaninglessness and similar self-defeating attitudes.

Organisational

The use of TA techniques within organisations for improving communications and for building interpersonal and leadership skills is well known. Many organisations are also running guided yoga and meditation classes for their employees with a view to relieving stress and promoting their all-round health. However, if we can combine the TA concepts with the philosophy behind practising yoga and meditation, as in the Vedantic Ego States Model, we get a ready mechanism in the Discriminating Intellect for exploring and determining one's values and formulating a personal code of conduct based on the principles of *Shreyas, Rin* and *Svadharma*. Appreciation of the worldview of *Vedanta* will add moral and ethical dimensions to business values, which is significant in these days of Values-Based Leadership and Spiritual Quotient.

The framework given by the Vedantic Model of Ego States can be used by itself or in conjunction with other TA models in order to improve interpersonal relationships, quality of communications and set up an OK-OK outlook within a team, a department or a company.

Educational

Within the existing educational applications of TA, the insights of *Vedanta* provide a way to guide young impressionable minds along the path of moral and ethical behaviour and right conduct. At the same time, the primacy accorded to the intellect can encourage young people to think out things for themselves, learn to discriminate, test their assumptions and formulate a humane worldview right from the start. As in the case of organisations, the Vedantic Ego States Model can be used either by itself or in conjunction with other models, to serve as a guide for developing and strengthening the intellect. In TA, the Adult is recognized to be ageless; this translates into the Vedantic model as the Intellect is ageless; and children from a young age can learn how to make the correct use of its various functions and attributes, if they are provided with the permissions appropriate to their stage of development.

Intellect versus Belief

Although the philosophy of *Vedanta* represents, in my opinion, a masterly creation of the human intellect, there are some things in it that are problematic, at least for me. I had remarked earlier that the ocean of *Vedanta* is vast, perhaps due to the inevitable mingling of spirituality with organised religion. I find some aspects of the philosophy, well, difficult to swallow. The most significant of these is the *Guna* theory of the personality, which is enshrined in the *Bhagavad Gita*. Simply put, it states that every human being's personality is composed of three inherent qualities called *sattva, rajas* and *tamas*, with one or the other dominant in a person. For example, a person who is predominantly *satvik* has a bias towards purity, harmony, balance, knowledge and intelligence; one who is predominantly *rajasic* is inclined to desire, energy, action, and movement; a *tamasic* personality is ignorant, lazy, dull and passive. This theory is then used to justify the fourfold division of human beings into the caste system, with the *satvik* Brahmin at the top of the hierarchy, the *rajasik* types as the *Kshatriyas* and *Vaishyas,* and the *tamasic* ones as the *Shudras*.

My intellect rejects this theory completely. I cannot digest a theory that implies some people are by nature slothful, some energetic, and some "pure", whatever that means. Still less can

I understand the use of this premise to differentiate among people. I prefer to believe with Berne that:

"Every child is born a prince or a princess..."

The science of Epigenetics, referred to in Chapter IX, also implies that the environment in which a child is brought up sends signals to the genes to make proteins accordingly that shape the child's personality. My belief is *that the only inherent quality in a newborn is "I'm OK, You're OK"*.

I do not know why this patently discriminatory theory came to be included in the otherwise sublime philosophy of *Vedanta*. Indeed, the mixing of philosophy and organised religion could have introduced considerations other than pure philosophical speculation. Organised religion is after all a man-made code of behaviour promising a reward to those who follow it, while *Vedanta* is essentially a search for connecting to a higher power. We do know that the established social order at that time was under threat because of the rising popularity of Buddhism and Jainism. Perhaps the *Guna* theory was a Brahminical device to solidify the caste system and reinforce their own place at the top of the ladder. There is a school of thought among Indian historians which holds that the *Bhagavad Gita* is a later addition to the *Mahabharata*, and further, it went through many additions, interpolations and revisions before reaching its final form. The answer may possibly be found there. However, it is beyond the scope of this book to speculate further on this issue.

And now that these candid observations are written down, it remains to pay willing homage to the power and profundity of the Vedantic conception. To my mind, it is a masterpiece of insight and intuition, unrivalled in its subtlety, scope and sheer grandeur. It embraces body, mind and soul, and shows us how to live a fulfilling and spiritually enriching life, in harmony with others and with the environment. A great poet has written:

"Ah, that a man's reach might exceed his grasp,
Or what's a Heaven for?"

—Robert Browning

With *Vedanta*, we grasp as high as we can reach, and learn the way to Heaven also.

Three Credos

The guiding lights that have inspired me all through are *Vedanta* and Transactional Analysis; both have changed my life in countless ways. To add flesh and blood to philosophy and psychology, there are three credos I try to live by, which I would like to share in the hope the reader may find them useful.

The first is a twist to the famous Serenity Prayer:

"God grant me the strength to accept
The people I cannot change,
The courage to change the one I can,
And the wisdom to know... it's me!"

The second: lyrics of a Leonard Cohen song, for once not enigmatic,

"I saw Jesus on a cross,
On a hill called Calvary
Do you hate mankind
For what they've done to you?
He said, Talk of love, not hate
Things to do, it's getting late
I haven't got much time,
And I'm only passing through"

—Leonard Cohen, Passing Through

The third is deeply personal; it is a rhyme my father taught me when I was a child, and it has stayed with me all through my life:

"My entry into this world
Was naked and bare
My journey through the world
Is full of trouble and care
My exit from this world
Will be nobody knows where
But if I do good here
I shall do well there"

References

Chapter I

1. Berne, Eric (1961), *Transactional Analysis in Psychotherapy*, New York: Grove Press
2. Berne, Eric (1964), *Games People Play,* New York: Grove Press
3. Berne, Eric (1972), *What Do You Say After You Say Hello?* New York: Grove Press
4. Holloway, William (1977), *Transactional Analysis: An Integrative View in Barnes, G. (ed) Transactional Analysis after Eric Berne: Teachings and Practices of Three TA Schools,* New York: Harper's College Press
5. Ohlsson, Thomas (1988), *A "Mandala Model" of the Adult Ego States Transactional Analysis Journal,* 18:1
6. De Luca, Maria Luisa & Tosi, Maria Teresa (2011), *Socio-Cognitive Transactional Analysis: An Introduction to Pio Scilligo's Model of Ego States Transactional Analysis Journal,* 41:3
7. Victoria Baskerville (2022), *A Transcultural and Intersectional Ego State Model of the Self: The Influence of Transcultural and Intersectional Identity on Self and Other, Transactional Analysis Journal,* 52:3
8. James, Muriel (1981), TA in the 80s: *The Inner Core and the Human Spirit, Transactional Analysis Journal,* 11:1
9. Chandran, Sashi (2007), *Connecting With the Guru Within: Supervision in the Indian Context, Transactional Analysis Journal*, 37(3)

10. Mellor, Ken (2008), *Autonomy With Integrity, Transactional Analysis Journa*l, 38(3)
11. Zvelc, Gregor, and Others (2011), *Mindfulness Based Transactional Analysis, Transactional Analysis Journal,* 41(3)
12. Sandle, Rod (2019), *Hidden in Plain Sight: Spirituality in Transactional Analysis, Transactional Analysis Journal,* 49(2)
13. Swami Parthasarathy (2000), *Vedanta Treatise,* Mumbai: Vedanta Life Institute
14. Tudor, Keith (2003), *The Neopsyche: The Integrating Adult ego state in C. Sills & H Hargaden (eds) Ego States.* London: Worth Publishing

Chapter II

1. Santoke, Janki (2019), *How Do You Know What You Know?* Mumbai: Janki Santoke
2. Berne, Eric (1964), *Games People Play,* New York: Grove Press
3. Berne, Eric (1961), *Transactional Analysis in Psychotherapy,* New York: Grove Press
4. Ohlsson, Thomas (1988), *A "Mandala Model" of the Adult Ego States Transactional Analysis Journal,* 18:1
5. Drego, Pearl (2000), *Toward an Ethic of Ego States Transactional Analysis Journal,* 30:3
6. Oller-Vallejo, Jorge (2002), *In Support of the Second-Order Functional Model. Transactional Analysis Journal,* 32:3
7. Oller-Vallejo, Jorge (2003), *Three Basic Ego States: The Primary Model Transactional Analysis Journal,* 33:2
8. De Luca, Maria Luisa & Tosi, Maria Teresa (2011), *Socio-Cognitive Transactional Analysis: An Introduction to Pio Scilligo's Model of Ego States, Transactional Analysis Journal,* 41:3
9. Rachel Cook (2023), *The Development of the Adult Self: An Existential, Relational, and Developmental Approach*

to Our Human Search for Meaning, Transactional Analysis Journal, 53:3

10. Easwaran, E. (1981), *Dialogue with Death: The Spiritual Psychology of the Katha Upanishad,* trans. Eknath Easwaran, Petaluma, California, Nilgiri Press.
11. Swami Rama (1996), *Perennial Psychology of the Bhagavad Gita,* Honesdale, Pennsylvania, Himalayan International Institute of Yoga Science and Philosophy
12. *The Upanishads,* trans. Paramahansa Yogananda, www.yogananda.com.au.
13. Chakraborty, S.K. (1995), *Ethics in Management: Vedantic Perspectives,* New Delhi: Oxford University Press
14. Mellor, K. (2008), *Autonomy with Integrity, Transactional Analysis Journal,* 38(3)
15. Servaas van Beekum & Bastianne Krijgsman (2000), *From Autonomy to Contact, Transactional Analysis Journal,* 30:1
16. Frankl, V. (1959), *Man's Search for Meaning*, New York: Washington Square Press.
17. Pearl Drego (1983), *The Cultural Parent, Transactional Analysis Journal,* 13(4)

Chapter III

1. *The Upanishads*, trans. Paramahansa Yogananda, www.yogananda.com.au.
2. Swami Vivekananda (1987), *Vedanta: Voice of Freedom,* Advaita Ashram, Kolkata
3. Will Durant (1926), *The Story of Philosophy*, New York: Simon and Schuster
4. Swami Prabhupada (1972), *The Bhagavad Gita As It Is*, New Delhi: ISKCON
5. *Great Dialogues of Plato,* trans. B. Jowett (1892), London: Oxford University Press
6. Guerriere, D. (1980), *Physis*, Sophia, Psyche. In J. Sallis & K. Maly (Eds.) *Heraclitean Fragments: A companion*

volume to the Heidegger/Fink Seminar on Heraclitus, Tuscaloosa, University of Alabama Press

7. Clarkson, P. *Physis in Transactional Analysis, Transactional Analysis Journal,* 22(4)
8. Cornell, W. (2010), *Aspiration or Adaptation? An Unresolved Tension in Eric Berne's Basic Beliefs, Transactional Analysis Journal,* 40(3-4)
9. Swami Parthasarathy (2000), *Vedanta Treatise,* Mumbai: Vedanta Life Institute

Chapter IV

1. Hay, J. (2009), *T.A. for Trainers,* Hertford, U.K. Sherwood Publishing
2. Rachel Cook (2022), *Connection, Hungers, and Time Structuring: A Relational, Inclusive, and Transpersonal Development of Autonomy, Transactional Analysis Journal*, 52(4)
3. Kandathil, G. and Kandathil, C. (1997), *Autonomy: Open Door to Spirituality, Transactional Analysis Journal,* 27(1)
4. Swami Vivekananda (1987), *Vedanta: Voice of Freedom*, Advaita Ashram, Kolkata
5. *The Upanishads*, trans. Paramahansa Yogananda, www.yogananda.com.au

Chapter V

1. Maslow, A.H. (1954), *Motivation and Personality (First ed.)* New York: Harper & Row.
2. Rachel Cook (2022), *Connection, Hungers, and Time Structuring: A Relational, Inclusive, and Transpersonal Development of Autonomy, Transactional Analysis Journal*, 52:4
3. Swami Vivekananda (1987), *Vedanta: Voice of Freedom,* Advaita Ashram, Kolkata
4. Keith Tudor (2011), *Understanding Empathy, Transactional Analysis Journal*, 41:1

5. Barrow, G., & Marshall, H. (2020), *Ecological transactional analysis—Principles for a new movement. The Transactional Analyst,* 10(2)
6. Will Durant (1926), *The Story of Philosophy,* New York: Simon and Schuster
7. Swami Rama (1996), *Perennial Psychology of the Bhagavad Gita,* Honesdale, Pennsylvania, Himalayan International Institute of Yoga Science and Philosophy

Chapter VI

1. Swami Rama (1996), *Perennial Psychology of the Bhagavad Gita*, Honesdale, Pennsylvania, Himalayan International Institute of Yoga Science and Philosophy
2. Robert Frost (1916), *Mountain Interval* New York: Henry Holt and Co.
3. Swami Vivekananda (1987), *Vedanta: Voice of Freedom,* Advaita Ashram, Kolkata
4. Immanuel Kant, *Groundwork of the Metaphysics of Morals*
5. Rudyard Kipling (1902), *Just So Stories*
6. *The Upanishads,* trans. ParamahansaYogananda, www.yogananda.com.au
7. Paul Reps (1957), *Zen Flesh, Zen Bones*
8. Joe Dispenza (2012), *Breaking the Habit of Being Yourself,* California: Hay House
9. Rudyard Kipling (1910), *If*

Chapter VII

1. Francis Bacon, (16th c. CE), *Novum Organum*
2. Drego, P. (1981), *The Cultural Parent, Transactional Analysis Journal,* 13(4)
3. *Complete Works of Swami Vivekananda,* Advaita Ashram, Kolkata
4. *Tales and Parables of Sri Ramakrishna Paramahansa*, Advaita Ashram, Kolkata

Chapter VIII

1. Aristotle, 4th c. BCE, *Essays*
2. Yogoda Satsang, 2023, *Annual Issue*
3. Swami Parthasarathy (2000), *Vedanta Treatise*, Mumbai: Vedanta Life Institute
4. *Complete Works of Swami Vivekananda*, Advaita Ashram, Kolkata
5. Paul Reps (1957), *Zen Flesh, Zen Bones*

Chapter IX

1. Gary Zukav (1979), *The Dancing Wu Li Masters*, New York: Morrow
2. Joe Dispenza (2012), *Breaking the Habit of Being Yourself*, California: Hay House
3. Bruce Lipton (2005), *The Biology of Belief*, UK: Hay House